I0669366

HEART OF FLAME

THE FIFTH CRYSTAL KINGDOM NOVEL

RAYMOND S FLEX

1

HOPE IN WAVES

W HEN RUTTERNESS had spotted the darkness settling down on the horizon, the night had seemed almost as if it would be a mercy. As if it might be something of a relief after the hard day of horse-riding Rut had just been through.

As it was, though, the darkness did nothing to mitigate the stifling heat.

If anything, the air became more humid.

It felt as if sweat oozed from every pore of his skin.

Thoroughly soaking his once-white cotton undershirt.

This morning, when Rut had set out from the tiny village he had stayed at the night before, the female proprietor of the inn—a real battle-axe who had clearly kept a very tightly run ship—had pointed him in this direction; the way to Almber's Bay, where Rut's journey would come to an end.

The battle-axe had told him that the shortcut to reach the sea was through a forest.

Well, Rut had come through the forest all right—and he had cuts and bruises all over his body to show for it—but there was still no sign at all of the coastline; let alone the sea. He had got it into his mind that the proprietor of the inn had deliberately deceived him.

He had learned well about the deceptiveness of strangers on his journey thus far . . .

It seemed as if Rut had seen off more than a dozen groups of robbers at this point. They had been somewhat surprised to find their rogue arrows fail to penetrate the armoured leather vest about his chest; and even more surprised still when they found, with a flash of silver, the blade of a sword splitting their skull. He knew that most robbers saw him as a prize catch; as a dough-shaped man on the back of an emaciated horse. But he had used that particular misconception against them; time and time again. He knew that the survivors of these melees would never take an overweight rider for granted in the future; no matter how easy the pickings looked.

Rut had put on the leather armour this morning; but he had tucked it away into one of the saddlebags after about five minutes' ride out of the village. The weather was simply too stifling.

The way he saw it, if somebody wanted him dead so badly, after he had come all this way, then they could have their wish.

It wasn't like he had anything to steal, either; he'd run through most of the funds which King Louson Dorf had given him for the journey. All that remained was his sword, his armour and his bedraggled-looking horse.

Perhaps the only solace of the day's ride had been that fruity smell on the breeze; an odour which he had never previously experienced. It reminded him a little of a bakery; the sweet smells which emanated from within; all those herbs and spices, and who knew whatever else.

And it seemed to come from all around him, wafting about on the cruelly baking-hot breeze. He was sure that he must stink of the scent now, and he vaguely wondered if he ever did reach the sea, whether he'd be able to find an inn which would be glad to put him up for the night. During his travels, he had seen journeymen turned away for all variety of reasons; sometimes because of a sordid appearance, or reputation, but just as often due to a lack of personal hygiene. Not that travellers, like Rut, really had much choice; he himself had had to camp out in the open at night, at times, unable to track down a nearby inn.

And if he didn't manage to reach the sea before the darkness fully smothered the world surrounding him, then Rut knew he would need to bed down in the open once again.

He stared about himself now.

The ground was lumpy and it had already caught Rut off guard several times; the dips in the terrain catching out his balance, and almost sending him tumbling off the side of his horse. When he glanced back over his shoulder, he could see no trace of the forest he had passed through on his horse that morning. All around him, the world was flat, and lumpy.

In many ways, it reminded him of where he had grown up; in Quagsmile, one of the Northern Villages—the villages to the north of Ilsnare. There the ground had been flat for miles around; all of it flattened for farmland, only the odd tree, here and there, by way of variation. It was difficult to believe that, at one time, those plains had been his entire life.

The grass was cut short here—grazing cattle?—and he could see large patches of sand protruding from between the gaps: a sort of deceptive promise that a sandy beach might be just around the corner.

Already, Rut found himself longing to experience a beach—to experience the *sea*. Ever since he had met Lou, he had found himself swept along on a wave of adventure. He had experienced the plains—*so much of the plains!*—and the foothills of the Sable Mountains. But, when he'd been en route to Onderswort, the prison colony, and to the coast which would provide his gateway there, Lou had—*thankfully*—broken him and Sulliman free.

Soon after Lou had been appointed King of Shellacnass, Rut had found himself appointed: Rutterness, Royal Guardian of the Waterways.

Ironically, though, this work hadn't allowed Rut so much as a single journey to the sea.

His work had maintained him, without exception, inland; mostly in helping to solve disputes between farmers, about who could do what with which irrigation.

To be honest, Rut had been glad when Lou had summoned him back to the Crystal City with the promise of something far 'meatier' for him to sink his teeth into.

The adventure he was on now.

As Rut rode onward, feeling the stiff muscles of his horse beneath him, and listening to its shallow breaths, he realised that he really was going to have to stop for the night out here. That he was going to need to give his horse a break.

Resigned to this fact, Rut swivelled on the saddle, and instantly felt a rush of blood to his head for his trouble. The heat really was getting to him more than he cared to admit. When Lou had first informed him that he would need to travel to the tropics, Rut had believed that it would be nothing save paradise . . . and perhaps it *was* that when there was no sense of urgency, when there weren't objectives to be taken care of; tasks to be completed.

Horses to be ridden.

Rut was hanging off the side of his horse when something caught the corner of his eye. He paused his motion, half having helped himself down from his horse. He was used to this time of day; when the darkness hadn't quite yet reached its fullest, and the sunlight continued to dribble out from over the horizon. It was a time that played tricks on the mind. Sometimes he fancied seeing things that weren't there at all.

Like he did now.

And yet, he was *certain*.

Realising that his horse was breathing heavily and, more than likely, about to keel over if he retained his current pose, he dropped down to the ground; feeling the welcoming springiness of the sandy earth beneath his feet.

Rut gazed off in the direction of the object which'd caught his attention.

He squinted hard, feeling the wrinkles form in his brow.

What *was* that?

The daylight had all but crept away now, and the darkness continued to drape itself over the entire landscape. And yet, just over there—just over the hill—Rut could make out something apparently metal glimmering away ... if a scrap of daylight hadn't continued to leak out across the world then Rut would've convinced himself that it was the reflection of the moon on something metal.

No matter how long Rut continued to stare at the object, he couldn't bring it any clearer.

As he continued to observe, he felt a bead of sweat drool down the side of his face. He reached up and swatted it away. He breathed in the musky scent of his own sweat, mixed up with dirt and sand. It'd been a long journey for him to get this far, and he knew that his mind had been worn down. He needed to take some time to rest. Some time out of the saddle.

His horse, too, would thank him for that.

And now, here he was, *seeing* things.

"Come on," Rut said, leading his horse by the reins, over to a spot in the terrain where the grasses were longer.

He recalled how, before he'd set off on this journey, his wife Emelda, had berated him *not* to become one of those madmen who started speaking with their horses when there was nobody else around to speak with. And although Rut had found his brain swilling with the oddness of the comment—for if there was no one to hear a madmen speaking with his horse then who would there be to tell about it?—he found his wife's words ringing true.

He vaguely wondered what his wife might make of his appearance right now. Last night, when he'd got a look at himself in a mirror at the inn, he'd noted how his blond hair was grimy, his cheeks engrained with dust and dirt which wouldn't be loosened with even near-scolding water. Even his light-blue eyes seemed to have sunk into a slightly mulchy-green shade.

Today, Rut had *really* hoped that it would be today.

That he'd manage to reach the sea.

But there was always tomorrow.

As Rut led his horse by the reins, toward the grassy spot, he could feel his stomach grumbling. He knew that there was precious little by way of supplies in the saddlebags.

Whatever remained would have to do.

Last night, in the inn, he had used the small amount of money which'd been left over to buy some more oats for his horse. Thankfully the well of drinking water around the back of the inn had been free for all guests to use.

Rut withdrew the leather bedroll which he had tied to the side of his horse, and laid it down on the ground. That done, he strapped the nosebag onto his horse and listened to the quiet sound of munching commence.

For himself there was only water.

He had finished the rest of the bread earlier in the day.

But Rut couldn't care less ... he had to rest now.

He needed to take a load off.

And, with one final look back to the horizon, searching for that flicker of light, Rut allowed himself to sink down onto his bedroll.

And to drift away into sleep.

2

INTRUDER

HILDIE WOKE WITH A START.

She heard voices chattering around her.

The sound of commotion that only an intruder could bring.

It was hot, and she'd hardly managed to drift away into sleep. She guessed that she'd been asleep for less than an hour. Her hut was made of rushes and held together with mud, and when she peered out through the mouldy material which hung down over the entrance, she saw that the sun had sunk beneath the horizon.

Night was here.

Today really had worn her out, and she hadn't been able to resist the comfort of the warm, soft straw which her hut had offered.

She could still feel the slightly dizzying effect of the berry wine she had taken that afternoon. The now-bitter taste of it at the back of her mouth; the smell of the roasting pork still clung to the tunic she hadn't bothered to change out of before falling into bed.

It had been a celebration, one of many which she hadn't quite yet managed to wrap her head around. She was a stranger in a strange land.

And yet, all at the same time, she felt as if she had come home.

Perhaps she was coming to terms with the fact that she would always be an outsider.

No matter where she went.

Slowly, her mind caught up with the language outside.

The people she was staying with were known as the Almber, and their language had the same name . . . as far as she knew.

It was a hurried, mumbled language which made little sense to her unless she could see the accompanying frenetic hand gestures.

But she managed to get by.

And their kindness toward her more than made up for the difficulties of communication.

She'd only arrived here a year or so ago, after wandering about much of the tropical region; like a lost lamb looking for the trusty shepherd who'd long ago passed on.

Or was it more like a lonesome she-wolf searching for her next hunk of meat?

Judging by the reaction of the Almber to outsiders—and their reaction to her from the start—she supposed that they had been just as unsure.

Hildie eased herself up onto her elbow, favouring her good right arm as she always did. It had become second-nature to hide the scarred stump of her left hand from sight wherever she went, and with whatever she did, even when alone. The stump which remained of her left hand was a battle scar, of sorts, and one which—despite the offers of several well-meaning wise women and mages along her journey—she had never seen reason to heal.

9

As she sat up on her bed of straw, she attempted to make sense of the shadows scurrying past her hut in the fledgling torchlight.

The hut was just about big enough for herself, and she was somewhat honoured that the Almber had seen fit to build her her own hut. Especially since those first few days, just about the first week of her stay with them, had been so fraught.

The only issue with the hut was that the Almber, in general, having a much squatter build, hadn't quite accounted for her size. She was a clear head and shoulders taller than even the largest of the men among them.

As it was, whenever Hildie stood up, she had to remind herself to bend over so that she wouldn't bump her head on the wooden rafters.

She often forgot.

As Hildie slipped out past the mouldy material hanging across the entrance, and onto the beach, she stared out at the placid sea.

Despite the situation, despite the obvious excitement rippling along the beach among the Almber, Hildie couldn't help but find herself attracted to the sea.

Being drawn in by it.

The moon was shining now, and its sallow light splashed across the surface of the water. She lost herself in a daze as she attempted to track the ever-changing shapes of the light; to try and find some sort of long-hidden meaning to them. Somebody had once told her that there were 'clues' in nature, that if a person could only learn to observe them then, why, the entire world would be their own.

The water swept in over the sandy beach, slick and smooth, and impossibly clear.

This was paradise, Hildie was certain.

This *was* paradise.

Now that night had fallen, Hildie felt a slight chill pass through her blood. She knew that it was the fire magic within her reacting; protesting against the night. She knew that it would've liked nothing better than to huddle down in the straw of her hut and snooze away . . . to wait for the flaming sun to rise again. Or, better still, for her to flop down beside one of the many campfires spread across the shore and feel the heat of the flames up against her skin.

But Hildie wouldn't give in to the whims of her magic.

She was better than that.

She had learned control.

These ten years in the wilderness—was it more?—had taught her so much, but, above all else, they had taught her how to make magic work for her; how she no longer needed to give in to the feeling of pain, or of pleasure. She could be just like any other walking, talking Mortal; her magic tucked away safely beneath the surface of her skin.

If only her father—Ma'reygar—could see her now.

He would've claimed that she had wasted her gift.

That she had allowed greatness to slip through her fingers.

But what if Hildie didn't aspire to 'greatness'?

What if she was happy with just what she was doing now?

What if she had already found her peace?

Hildie turned away from the quietly lapping waves and looked over the beach.

First, as always, she found her attention drawn in by the glittering sand; the golden dust among the ordinary grains which reflected the light from the torches. She had done her best to ask after this effect, but, since her communication skills weren't entirely up to scratch, she hadn't got anything near a satisfactory explanation. Needless to say, though, the sight was quite something.

She peered up from the sand and to the Almber villagers, all of them—men, women and children—standing and looking off into the distance. Their forms silhouetted by the torches planted in a scattered manner across the shore. The torchlight bounced about the sand, becoming entangled with the refreshingly cool night-time breeze.

Already, Hildie could feel the tug of her fire magic, imploring her to get closer to the flames, for her to bask in the warmth. But she told herself that she couldn't give in; that she couldn't submit to its whim . . . although *that* task was made all the easier by the sense of curiosity which ripped through the air.

She followed the group gaze, over to the grassy sand dunes which led off to the plains beyond; and back to civilisation. Even the thought of civilisation—even the thought of *going back*—sent a shudder down Hildie's spine.

She no longer *wanted* civilisation.

And she was certain civilisation no longer wanted her.

Which was why invaders—although she had been one herself, at the start—made her feel greatly uneasy.

She scanned the indigenous-looking faces of the Almber, struck somewhere between apprehension and excitement. She took in the ragged clothing which just about covered up the more sensitive parts of their body. Bronzed skin which glittered slightly in the torchlight; the golden dust which'd rubbed onto their bodies from their day-to-day lives living upon the sands.

She wondered how many had stumbled across the Almber before, and how many had underestimated them.

She knew that she—*herself*—had done just that.

But she pushed that thought away for the time being.

And turned her attention back onto the Almber, and the approaching scouting group.

There were about half a dozen Almber, all of them females, as was the custom.

Although it had struck Hildie as somewhat odd that the women were the ones who would head out on expeditions, who would keep track of their surroundings while the men tended to the fires, and to the fishing, and to the care of the children; she had eventually realised that it made a great deal of sense.

While the male members of the Almber tended to be squat and muscular, seemingly made to be warriors; the female members were far more slender. What Hildie had most noted was how Almber women learned to be silent about their movements; how they could make their way across the beach without raising so much as a single sound.

The men, on the other hand, seemed a never-ending source of grunts or chitters or barks.

Their job, as Hildie understood it from her short stay so far, was to stay behind.

To defend the village.

She recalled the many spears she had found thrust in her face when she had first been treated as an invader; and she often caught sight of them kept concealed beneath huts, apparently out of all-but-the-most-curious of children's reach.

Some of the men, apparently having left behind the afternoon's indulgences of berry wine, had snapped to their senses and were desperately on their hands and knees digging about beneath huts for their spears.

Hildie trudged her way between the stunned members of the Almber; feeling as if, for the first time, she wasn't the focus of attention.

When she'd first come here—when she'd first been let free—she could recall how men, women and children had hardly stopped staring at her brilliant red hair, with a few strands of grey here and there. How they never ceased to be captivated by her fair, freckled skin.

Once a child—a girl—had approached her during the day, looking extremely wary, and although Hildie hadn't understood her thickly intoned words, she'd comprehended the gestures as the girl pointed at her eyes . . . apparently seeking some explanation for the green eyes Hildie had; and which none of the Almber seemed to possess.

She hadn't been able to explain, of course; and she wondered, even if she and the girl had shared a common language, if she would have known how to reply.

She had never had children—there had hardly been a moment to consider it—and it seemed she had lost all of the abilities and techniques she might once have possessed to relate to them.

She focussed in on the approaching group of women, and then to the person who they held between them. Already, Hildie could see that it was a man; about her age, maybe a few years older, give or take. She saw how he looked a little wilted, his clothes seeming to hang off him; and she supposed that he had been much larger before he had commenced his journey . . . whatever journey that had been.

It was only as the women brought the man between them, his

neck neatly fitted into a loop of rope at the end of a wooden plank, that she got a proper look at his face.

At the *man's* face.

Hildie's eyes locked with his.

And a spark tickled Hildie's stomach.

They recognised one another.

It took several more moments before Hildie could supply a name—it *had* been at least ten years since she had seen anybody associated with Ilsnare.

Rutterness.

Or, simply, 'Rut' as he referred to himself.

Just as she referred to herself as Hildie, instead of Hilda.

3
———
HOLE

HILDIE WATCHED ON as they took Rut away from her, and toward the shoreline. With Rut still held on the end of the wooden plank, with the rope around his neck, they lowered him down onto his knees and formed a circle about him; apparently so that he would have no hope of escape.

She wondered where he might run to; Hildie hadn't any idea where the closest town or village to this spot might be . . . and, to tell the truth, all that she hoped was that it was *far* away.

She could already see that the male members of the Almber were digging a hole in the sand.

She felt her mind switch back to when she had arrived here.

It had been at night too.

She recalled very clearly staring across the sandy beach, with its glittering, golden sands . . . the dust which actually *did* glitter in the moonlight. And then she had looked back out across the sea, and thought to herself that a slight alcove in the glittering sand dunes would be the perfect place for her to bed down for the night.

She had been entirely unaware of the village just around the corner.

Sometimes she wondered what might've been if she hadn't dropped herself down into the glittering sand and slipped off to sleep. She wondered if the men of the village would've simply raised their spears to her—seen her as a threat straight away—and killed her where she stood.

She could tell, even from that snatched look at Rut's face, that they had come across him while he had been sleeping. He had had the bleariness of a long day's journey sketched all across his cheeks, and his eyes had had that unfocussed, dreamy look to them.

And now, if he didn't make some sort of move soon—if *Hildie* didn't make some sort of move soon—he would be dead.

The men were quick about digging out the hole and, she knew, from the games which the boys played on the beach from a young age, how they would all form a line and see who might be quickest to dig out a hole that they could fit themselves in; that this was a well-practised—and well-*prized*—skill.

Hildie supposed that the men managed to dig out the hole in less than a couple of minutes.

A hole which would accommodate Rut.

She stood back from the rest of the Almber, still feeling bleary from sleep herself, and still feeling a little numbed at what had happened—and *how* this had happened . . . how Rut had managed to *find* her.

The women, still with the rope about Rut's neck, led him over to the hole, and then, with Rut lingering on the edge, they slipped the noose quickly over the top of his head and—one of the women working faster than Hildie could fathom—shoved him neatly inside.

Hildie overheard a dampened, "Oof!" come from the hole.

She felt her gut clench tightly.

Suddenly she felt a hot sensation jab her temples.

At first, she believed that one of the Almber had sidled up beside her, in their typically silent way, and prodded her with their fingers. Why they might've done this, she had no idea. Perhaps it was the memory . . . her own memories . . .

But then she realised it had been her fire magic; no doubt protesting at her being out in the moonlight when there were torches and campfires to be had further up the beach.

The men formed a circle about the hole, and the women who had brought Rut back to the village broke away from their prisoner; their work—*apparently*—done.

Hildie continued to stare at the men who encircled Rut and she wondered what she might be able to do. She was conscious of so many things.

The first of them, of course, saw her fixated on what Rut was doing here . . . *why* he had come here, and under whose orders.

No matter how much Hildie might've *liked* Rut in the past, she knew that he was a follower not a leader; and that there would almost certainly be somebody behind him.

The second was, if Hildie did decide that she wanted to break Rut free of the impromptu gaol cell he'd found himself entrapped in, that she would struggle to communicate this desire to the Almber. Although she could just about get by in their language as far as 'Good Day' or 'Thank you' went, she knew ahead of time that it would be a struggle for her to get to grips with something more ethereal.

With something which demanded greater control.

As Hildie considered this, she felt the touch of one of the Almber women on her forearm.

Hildie turned to look. The woman entwined her fingers about her own. She squeezed Hildie's hand tightly, sending a welcome warmth flowing through her blood. The Almber woman smiled faintly at her and began to lead her away from the scene, from the sand gaol.

Hildie resisted for the first couple of seconds, but the Almber woman was insistent and much stronger than her diminutive height might've suggested.

Unable to do anything to resist, Hildie felt the Almber woman leading her away from the gaol, and back toward her hut.

Finally, when Hildie had taken maybe half a dozen steps, she turned her back on the sand gaol.

She turned her back on Rut.

He was on his own now.

Whatever he had come here to do, it was beyond *her* responsibility.

4

DREAMS OF FLAME

A LL AROUND HER, Hildie could feel the sand.
    She breathed in.
Could feel its gritty texture at the back of her throat.

Its grim, bitter taste on her tongue.

The dampness of it on all sides.

Pressing up against her skin.

She opened her eyes.

Black.

Everything was black.

But the worst thing . . . the *very worst thing* was the silence.

It felt as if sand stuffed her eardrums.

Blocking out all sounds.

And then, when she jerked her head upward, to take in the opening of the hole more than three times her body length above her head, she felt all her muscles tighten up. Her throat constricted.

She felt herself draw breath into her lungs, preparing to scream.

But when she opened her lips to make the sound, nothing came out.

Only the very quietest of whispers.

A tiny, echoless prayer for help.

But no one was coming . . . no one was coming for her . . . she would die here . . . in this hole . . . so far from everything she'd ever known; everything she'd ever *loved* . . . as she felt the world of darkness begin to swarm her vision, and to steal away the rest of her senses, her heart dropped down in her chest.

And she thought she must die.

It was then that she turned her attention upward.

To the opening of the hole.

And she saw the silhouette there.

Blocking out the moonlight.

She squinted—*screwed up her eyes.*

It was hard to make them out . . . hard to make out precisely who it was.

Her head ached.

Her heart ached.

Her stomach ached . . . her *whole body* ached.

And then she saw the rope as it was hurled into the hole.

She didn't dare remove her focus from the frayed strands.

She just stared at the minor miracle before her.

Then she reached out.

Gripped the gnarled rope with all her strength.

Planted her feet into the sides of the sandy pit.

Hauled herself upward.

And *out* . . .

Finally . . . *finally* . . . she was sure that she was getting herself free.

She was about half of the way to escaping the sandy hole when she thought to glance up again. To look to the figure who'd thrown in the rope which would save her life. The sight itself almost caused her to allow the rope to slip through her fingers.

But she—*somehow*—held on.

The figure . . . how he—she . . . *it?*—glowed.

That faint, deep orange.

As if flames glistened across the surface of the skin.

Hildie remained where she was, and then, before she could do anything to prevent it, she felt her grip failing her on the rope. Her muscles, unworked for weeks and weeks now, finally give out on her when she most needed them.

And she fell down.

Back to the bottom of the hole.

She stared back up above her.

To that glittering figure.

The one who'd thrown her the rope.

The one who'd tried to help her *escape.*

But now they'd gone.

And all that remained were the twinkling stars above.

The crisp, clean . . . *bitterly painful* . . . moonlight.

But there'd been hope too.

Hope that she could escape.

If only she put her mind to it.

And accepted a helping hand when it was offered.

5

AWAKE

HILDIE GASPED AT THE AIR.
But it just wouldn't enter her lungs.

It wouldn't do her any good.

She gulped and gulped and gulped, trying to get it down into her.

But the whole world swilled.

A world set in gloom; sporadically lit by the orange glow of night-time torches.

She stumbled away from the straw where she had lain.

Standing at the entrance to her hut, feeling the damp and mouldy material blow up against her skin, she could still feel the dream. She could still feel herself trapped. Back in that sand gaol . . . just as Rut was now.

The terror stayed with her.

She knew that it would never go away.

Not completely.

Some experiences—*traumatic experiences*—could never truly be left behind.

She could see the glimmer of daybreak on the horizon. The sun would soon return to wash its warm, cleansing rays across the beach. Already, she could feel the thrum of fire throughout her veins, wishing to kick her into activity. Her magic relished the prospect of being allowed to go free.

She glanced back into her hut, and then to her sad collection of possessions; nothing much more than screwed-up, unwashed clothing. There hadn't been any need for her to have possessions once she'd left civilisation behind and—to be honest—she had expected that death wouldn't ever be far away . . . that soon she would leave this world behind, go to join her father in the next one; whatever that turned out to be.

She padded across the creaking floorboards of the hut, feeling the familiar, natural grain of the wood against the bare soles of her feet.

She stooped over her bundled-up clothing, then dug through the materials, turning the articles over in her hands as if she was searching for something so simple as an outfit for the day ahead.

But she wasn't looking for an outfit.

Finally, she uncovered the vial; sleek glass with a cork jabbed into the top.

She gripped the vial tightly in her right fist and inspected the colourless, transparent liquid within. Then, still on her haunches, she turned herself around. She held the vial up to the fledgling daylight. The sun's rays twinkled in through the glass. Slowly, but surely, the liquid within lost its colourless consistency.

At first it seemed to take on a sort of silty-blue glow . . . the liquid glittering out from within. Then it became easier to predict.

She watched on as the liquid turned a pale-blue colour. And then came the bitter chill up against the glass.

It stung her palm.

She sunk her teeth into her lower lip.

Trying to cope with the sudden sensation.

No matter how many times she did this—how many times she went through *this* routine—she always found the result was the same . . . and yet she never grew accustomed to the sensation.

That was good . . . Hildie was glad . . . that was the whole *point* of the exercise.

All about control.

All about her controlling her fire magic.

She had to walk with weakness.

Show herself that—even here—a supposed safe haven for her magic, couldn't be thought of in those terms; not if she wanted to maintain control over her abilities.

So that she wouldn't turn out like her father.

Not like Ma'reygar.

Once she had finished with the exercise, she replaced the glass vial infested with ice magic among her scrunched-up clothes then yanked off the tunic she'd worn to bed the night before, replacing it with a floaty dress; one which she had been wearing during the celebrations last night.

It was feather-white, and floated down to her shins.

Living on the beach made it impractical to wear either shoes or trousers at any time. So she always opted for the lightest-weight clothing she could get away with.

Dressed, Hildie ventured out of the hut.

There were some of the Almber already out in the shallows, fishing with the morning tide. And she could also see that there was a group standing guard over the sand gaol, where they had thrown Rut the night before.

Hildie wondered if she should just go back into her hut.

If she should go back to sleep.

See if Rut's arrival had simply been a bad dream.

But standing here, right now, feeling the fresh morning breeze up against her cheeks, and hearing the sea slosh in and out, she knew that she was wide awake.

And that she would have to face Rut sooner or later.

As she trod through the sand, she was aware of the wily eyes of the guards—all men bearing spears—fixed on her. She was certain that they had made the link between herself and Rut; even from just their similarly toned complexions. Although Hildie knew that it'd be near impossible for her to explain something about the wider world to the Almber; that just because her and Rut's complexions matched it didn't mean they were from the same area of the world.

Except that she and Rut *were* from the same area.

Ilsnare.

At least that was what her father had always told her.

One of the males made a guttural grunt. She noted his grip squeeze his spear a little tighter. The blood leave his knuckles as he prepared for . . . she didn't know what . . .

Although she saw herself as having been accepted by the Almber, she had to be realistic, and remind herself that, only a matter of months ago, she had been in a hole just like the one Rut found himself in now.

Hildie decided that she needed to press her luck; for all that she knew there might be more of them, with Rut, and she owed it to the Almber to warn them, so that they could put up their defences. So that Hildie wouldn't be the one responsible for bringing destruction to their idyllic village . . . heavens knew that she had already wracked more than enough destruction in her life; and all she hoped for now was peace and quiet.

And perhaps even a chance to be forgiven.

Now she really was dreaming . . .

To Hildie's surprise, other than the one guard grunting and groaning at her, not one of the Almber made a move to prevent her peering in over the edge.

She saw Rut sitting at the bottom of the pit.

Legs crossed.

Head bowed.

Arms tucked up to his chest.

He was wearing the same undershirt and riding trousers he'd been escorted to the village in the night before; though why the Almber would've allowed a wardrobe change escaped her.

Hildie felt a shudder pass through her heart as she recalled how the mornings had felt; how an almost icy chill had crept into that hole while she had sat there . . . and how there would only be a few hours of pleasant warmth before the hole became unbearably hot; even for her fire magic.

"Rut?" she said, calling down into the hole, her words almost seeming to be absorbed by the sandy sides.

Rut remained still for several moments, and she wondered if he'd heard her at all.

She recalled how, after the first few days she'd spent down in the hole, her mind had begun to get away from her. And how she'd found all sorts of dizzy thoughts filling her brain.

Rut finally tilted his head upward and looked at her with bleary eyes.

His face still had the doughy quality to it, but she could see that it'd become withered following what must've been a treacherous and lengthy journey.

Although his skin was surely flayed a sun-burn red, from where Hildie stood, on the edge of the hole, she could see that his complexion was far closer to being a blue-purple sort of hue. And she knew that the night-time, near-freezing conditions had taken their toll.

Hildie straightened up, looked to the guards, their spears still in their hands, and all of them with their eyes fixed on her. She told them the Almber words for 'food' and 'water', and then, after several swift repetitions, one of the guards set off traipsing across the sands.

She was well aware of the remaining guards' stare upon her.

But she pushed it to the edge of her mind and turned her attention downward, to Rut at the bottom of the sand gaol. When she spoke again, she surprised herself with her slightly venomous tone. Perhaps a decade and more hadn't been long enough for certain wounds to heal. "Why've you come here?" she said.

Rut remained still, without replying.

He was squinting up at her, and clearly still having trouble in fathoming the course of events which'd led to his current predicament.

"Who *sent* you here?" Hildie said, following up her first question and hoping to draw an answer out of him at last.

But all that Rut could summon by way of reply was a rasping sound at the back of his throat.

Another of the guards mumbled something to her in Almber.

And although Hildie didn't grasp the subtle tones of meaning of his words, she did understand completely the tip of his spear pointed at her chest.

She glanced back down into the sand gaol, hoping to hear *something* from Rut's lips, but it seemed that he was at the end of his wick. That he would need some time to himself so that he might have a chance to recuperate his strength.

She shifted her attention to her surroundings, realising that all the remaining guards were looking somewhat alert now; and with those spears in their hands too.

She needed to extricate herself from this situation for her own good.

Again, she cursed Rut having come here; no doubt *Lou* interfering once again . . . just the name of Louson Dorf, self-proclaimed King of Shellacnass, set off a fresh wave of ire throughout her whole body. He was so much like her, and yet look where he had ended up.

A *king* . . . while here *she* was . . . what?

An *outcast*?

. . . Yes, that was probably the best way to put it.

She was surprised at how easy it was to walk away from Rut; to leave him behind in that sand gaol of his to be well and truly tended to by his hosts.

All Hildie hoped was that he would simply disappear from this whole situation.

If that meant his death, then so be it.

As Hildie trod back over the threshold of her hut, she felt a strangely familiar smirk cross her lips and she supposed that, even after all these years, her mean streak had never quite deserted her.

She supposed that her father's blood still ran in her veins.

That Ma'reygar's blood still ran through her veins.

6

A LONG WAY FROM HOME

THE HEAT WAS NEARLY UNBEARABLE.

Rut had been sitting down in this sand gaol for the entirety of the day; for the entirety of the afternoon, and it was only now that he felt the sun's strength waning. Only now that he could sense dusk on the horizon did he feel any sort of optimism —optimism which was quickly curtailed by the realisation that night would soon be upon him and the freezing-cold conditions would descend once more.

How he'd made it through the previous night was something of a mystery.

While he'd been slumped down here, at the bottom of the hole, clutching his knees up to his chest, attempting to brew some sort of warmth in his blood, he decided that it'd been the thought of having seen Hildie; of having come *so close* to achieving his objective—the one which Lou had given him—which had allowed him to pull through.

And then he'd seen her again, in the morning light, peering down at him—*speaking to him* . . . and yet he'd been unable to find the words. His whole body had been rippling with fatigue—was *still* rippling with fatigue—and he hadn't even had the strength to so much as mumble a reply.

Soon after, the Almber had brought him food and water, and Rut had partaken of both with a great appetite and enormous thirst.

Only when he'd got through with both did he realise that he would be facing off with the baking-hot day down here, in this hole.

He wondered if this was a test . . . if the Almber were *testing* his resilience.

Did they expect him to die here?

That was something he'd heard in the inn—in that battle-axe's place—the night before.

About how the Almber dug holes . . . and threw their prisoners inside . . .

He could still recall the smile smeared all over the woman's mouth as she had declared that the prisoners found a way to clamber their way out or died.

Somehow, Rut felt as if he didn't have strength for either.

Even now, he could hardly make sense of what had happened.

The whole world spun before his eyes.

It had all happened so quickly.

He had sensed them, all around, while he'd been drifting in and out of the first stages of sleep. But he'd only thought to open his eyes when he'd smelled blood on the stilted air.

When he had sat up, he'd instantly felt the noose slip down over his head, and tighten about his neck. The bite of the rough strands against his skin. They'd tightened it almost to the point where he couldn't breathe; although he'd supposed that to be the point.

They had wanted to show their dominance over him.

That he was *their* prisoner.

And Rut, in that moment, had had no intention of arguing with them.

In his role as the Royal Guardian of the Waterways, he'd learned well that arguing over semantics never got you anywhere at all fast . . . except, maybe, into a physical conflict.

When they'd shunted him up to his feet, he had almost stumbled right over.

He wondered what might've happened if he had lost his balance.

Perhaps he would've choked to death; the rope tightening about his throat and strangling the life out of him.

Or maybe it would've been faster—maybe he would've been *lucky*—and the rope would've been so tight that it would've snapped his neck like the proverbial twig.

He'd seen, from the glow of their torchlight, that they'd taken his horse and slit open its throat.

That had explained the stink of blood in the air.

He had, of course, heard about these people—about the Almber—from the inn where he'd stayed the night before. The battle-axe, among others, had told him all about how the Almber shunned horses. From what Rut had gathered, the Almber had little use for them since they had no intention of leaving Almber's Bay behind. They lived off their own land so, in their eyes, matters such as commerce—or 'one-upmanship', as his father might've termed it—were beyond their aspirations.

It had been the overriding opinion at the battle-axe's inn that Rut should do whatever he possibly could to steer clear of the Almber; that he should make a point of taking a detour around Almber's Bay so that he wouldn't run into such an 'unpleasant, unwashed' people . . . the battle-axe's words, not his.

They were notably hostile toward outsiders; so much so that only a handful of those who'd been foolish enough to pay them a visit had ever escaped with their lives.

Had managed to escape from their gaols.

Rut recalled, too, how the battle-axe had asked him whether he was interested in the gold dust which, apparently, was the main attraction for the Almber's ill-fated visitors.

She had told him that the sandy beach was strewn with it; with dust which twinkled in the light from torches and the moon.

Rut supposed that, under other circumstances, if he hadn't so clearly found himself a prisoner of the Almber, he might've had some sort of chance to marvel at the spectacle.

As it was, though, the glittering, golden sands which'd swept all around him on either side had presented him with only a vague spark in his mind.

He had been *far* more concerned about the sharp tips at the ends of the spears, which every Almber seemed to possess.

As Rut sat down in the sandy pit—his *gaol*—he stared up at the darkening sky, and to the twinkling stars which'd just commenced to appear from the blackening canvas above.

He thought a lot about his wife; about Emelda. And then he thought about their home; their daughter, Forre. He had had everything there. The family around him which it had taken a lifetime to acquire, and which, in darker days, he would never have thought possible.

He knew, without having to admit it consciously to himself, that if it'd been anybody else apart from Louson Dorf who'd requested that he make this journey, he would've wasted no time in telling them where to stuff it . . . but it *had* been Lou . . . and there was no way he could possibly find a way to turn *Lou* down.

And so here he was now.

For better or worse.

In life.

Or in death.

7

NIGHT-TIME CAMPFIRES

HILDIE SAT DOWN on the log, beside one of the many campfires which sprouted into life sometime around dusk each and every night. She had put on a thick, woollen jumper over the top of her dress, to help ward off the cold. With the night coming in, and the moon appearing overhead, she felt her fire magic prickling about her body; setting off an itching sensation just beneath the surface of her skin . . . what she wouldn't do to be rid of her magic for good, if there ever might be a way to do so.

There was *one* way.

But she didn't feel quite up to it.

Not yet.

. . . *Death.*

Across the width of the beach—of the village—she noted the bodies all glittering with that same bronze, gold sparkle; their skins all caught by the moonlight. When Hildie turned her attention downward, onto herself, she noted how she, too, had begun to glitter a little . . . perhaps some time later she would glitter just as the Almber did.

Hildie listened to the crackling of pork flesh on the flames, mixed up with the salty scent of fish frying. She observed one of the male members of the Almber working hard on rubbing some spices into the meaty innards of the silver fish which'd been caught that morning. She still hadn't quite got to grips what exactly it was that the Almber did to make their dinners so delicious . . . sometimes she wondered, a little dizzily, whether she might be able to learn; that truly *would* be a spectacular skill to take with her back to civilisation.

But she wasn't *going* back to civilisation . . .

That thought hung in her mind, and she turned her attention toward the hole; to where Rut was being held prisoner.

As she turned her head, she caught sight of the beautiful, glittering dust embedded in the sand once more. It worked almost as a counterpoint to the sparkling stars in the night-time sky. A sort of brilliant, glistening bronze to the stars' elegant silver shine.

Hildie could see how it was possible for the Almber to never even entertain the *concept* of leaving Almber's Bay behind.

This *was* paradise . . . at least for the few who might be allowed to remain . . .

As Hildie took in the hole, the guards still standing sentry about the periphery, she found herself imagining just how Rut might be feeling at that moment in time. She had tried her best to stay occupied throughout the day, to force her mind away from thinking about Rut . . . or why he had come. The truth of the matter, if she admitted it to herself, was that Rut would die here. She was somehow convinced of the fact that he wouldn't be able to escape; he wouldn't get given the same helping hand that she had been given. Nobody would be coming to rescue *him*.

Hildie studied her emotions surrounding this fact.

She felt something—*of course, she felt something*—they had been through a great deal together in the past . . . but the past was just that . . . it was gone and couldn't be retrieved; whatever that might mean: good or bad.

The most dominant emotion Hildie experienced was a wild sense of curiosity.

More than anything else she decided, she would like to know exactly *what* . . . or should that be *who*? . . . had decided to send Rut here.

To where she had believed herself so well hidden.

She hardly knew where she was herself.

But that could wait until morning . . . or until a few days later; if Rut even managed to survive that long. She wasn't about to put her own life on the line in order to get answers to questions that didn't even matter any longer.

She was barely still in the Kingdom of Shellacnass.

She only clung to the very fringes of the frontier.

What did Louson Dorf have to do with her these days, after all this time?

. . . And, more to the point, why couldn't she shift Lou from her mind?

Sometimes she hated the Mortal body she'd been born with; sometimes she wondered if she might've been a better fit to have been born as some kind of a Creature.

Hildie felt as if her tongue was melting in her mouth as she eyed the male member of the Almber serving out her portion of fish. The Almber didn't believe in eating during the day—not even a snack here or there. They saved their appetites for when the sun went down. Thankfully, though, the evening meals were something akin to feasts, and Hildie fancied she eaten a hundred times her own weight in fish and pork since she'd been here.

And all of it deliciously seasoned.

Spiced to just the right level.

So that it brought sweat to her brow, and a tingle throughout her gut.

As Hildie accepted the fish—wrapped up in a large leaf; the tree of which Hildie couldn't identify—she noted the oddly percussive sound on the breeze.

She lifted her head to look, and saw that all the other members of the village; every single member of the Almber, without exception, had also lifted their heads to look.

It took Hildie another few seconds for her mind to feed her the conscious interpretation of just what those sounds signified.

8

HORSES

H ILDIE TUNED HER MIND into the constant *rumble* of
hooves.

Horses.

And they were moving quickly.

At a gallop.

The sound put her in mind of a cavalry gearing up for war;
charging the foot soldiers.

Only now the foot soldiers were the Almber.

And she was among them.

Hildie rose to her feet as she was dimly aware of the Almber
all ditching their dinner, allowing their fish or pork to drop at
their feet as they rushed for the huts; to locate their spears. She
also watched on as the male members of the Almber took care to
guide their women and children in beneath the huts; where they
would, apparently, be safe for the duration of the raid . . . because
that was what this was—*wasn't it?*

Hildie felt her entire body stirring with fire magic now, and she could feel the sparks at her fingertips, that relentless *pumping* sensation which implored her to let go.

Implored her to allow her magic free.

But not yet.

None of these people—none of the Almber—were aware of her powers; and she was fairly certain that the day she chose to show them just what she was capable of would be the last day she would be accepted among them.

She would need to move on again.

And, after these ten years, she was growing somewhat weary of perpetual travel.

She had hoped to stay here a while.

Although several of the Almber men attempted to gesture her down beneath the huts, so that she might be safe among their own women and children, Hildie managed to evade their grasp. And, as the men all rushed toward the direction of the stampeding hooves, Hildie found herself among the last to be standing in the village.

At first, she remained focussed on the men, all of the disappearing into the gloom which surrounded the village, making for the direction of the approaching horses; clearly hoping that they might be able to launch some sort of an ambush.

Then, when she came to the conclusion that she *needed* to move off her spot if she wasn't to make herself a duelling mannequin for the approaching horsemen, she ventured off in the direction of the hole where Rut was located.

In her panic, with her heart beating hard against her throat, she almost toppled right over the edge. Even though that particular eventuality didn't come to pass, she felt herself shudder all through her body at the simple thought of it.

She was determined that she wouldn't . . . that she *couldn't* . . . go back in there.

She stared down into the blackness of the pit and held her voice to a whisper. "Rut?" she said. "Rut?"

There was a stirring down in the pit.

And then she heard a reply.

"Hildie?" he said.

"Can you hear them?" Hildie replied. "Can you hear the horses?"

There was a long pause and then Rut answered, "That's what they are?"

Hildie straightened up, and stared off into the gloom surrounding the village. The men hadn't taken torches with them, of course, that would only have broadcast their location to the approaching enemy.

A sudden thought struck her.

She turned her attention downward once more.

To the hole.

To Rut below her.

Her voice felt unsteady and weak, but she did her best to make herself heard over the advancing beats of horses' hooves. "Is this anything to do with you?" she said. "Did *Louson* send along a whole cavalry to cover your tracks?"

Another pause, and then, "No," came the reply.

Hildie felt her entire body welling with fire magic now. She could feel the blood pumping up to her head. It wouldn't take much for her to boil over . . . for her to let loose a hex which would light up the night's sky. Even just thinking about it, she imagined how that sort of light might affect the Almber's bodies—how it would send the bronze-gold dust glistening all over their skin.

She glanced back to the village, and although she couldn't make out the shadows beneath the huts, she was certain that many of the villagers' eyes were upon her.

Thinking quickly, she turned back to Rut. "I'm sorry about this," she said, "but Lou's sent you to your death—there's nothing I can do for you. I *can't* save you. This is my home for the time being; this's where I've been *hiding out*." As she finished up that thought, she decided to add, under her breath, "Supposedly."

From within the hole, Hildie was certain that she heard a chuckle, though she couldn't be sure that it wasn't just the *thud* of horse's hooves over the sandy earth which surrounded Almber's Bay.

"Hildie?"

She turned her attention downward, into the hole; and she was sure that she could make out Rut skulking there in the darkness. It was incredible what sorts of details she could make out once her eyes grew accustomed to the dark . . . she supposed that this was the sort of ability which ice magic afforded those lucky enough to have it running in their veins.

But Hildie had been born with fire.

"What?" Hildie shot back in reply.

"You can't let me die."

It wasn't the words which took Hildie off guard, it was the matter-of-fact manner with which Rut had spoken. She wondered if he was going to shoot off into some sobbing explanation about how he had a wife and children—as far as she knew he did—and how he couldn't possibly leave *them* behind . . . but, as Hildie had found from her own childhood, there was nothing about an *untraditional* childhood which would keep a truly passionate, *determined*, boy or girl from their destiny.

Indeed, as it had done, in the case of her mother's death, it might only spur them on to find 'greatness' for themselves.

The *throb* of horses' hooves was so loud and the horses had come so close that she could now feel the vibrations passing through the sand at her feet. They would soon come to swarm the village; once they had managed to break through the line of male defenders.

She had to *do* something . . . and yet she could hardly hear herself think.

"You can't kill me," Rut said, his voice still giddy—and Hildie supposed it was from the sort of madness which set in after a day in the sun without food or water—"Without me, the location of the Webbing Armoury will be lost forever."

9

BREACHED

HILDIE CAUGHT SIGHT of the first Almber retreating into the village, his spear hanging down at his thigh, his other hand grasping his shoulder as blood poured freely down his muscular abdomen. He was panting heavily and staggering about.

Apparently exhausted, he came to a sudden halt, cried out long and hard—and *blood-curdling*—before dropping to his knees.

Falling flat on his face.

Dead.

Hildie held herself very still.

Her heart rapped against her ribcage.

She watched on as more and more of the Almber emerged from the gloom, all of them fleeing to the village, and the sound of the horses' hooves louder than it had been at any other time. It felt almost as if somebody was rapping their fists against Hildie's skull.

She crouched down by the hole, knowing that if she was going to save Rut's life then this was—*surely*—the time.

She dangled her good right hand down into the hole, using the stump of her left hand to support the rest of her weight on the other side, and then she called out to him. "Grab hold!" she said.

She waited to feel Rut's stubby fingers clutch hers.

But the sensation never arrived.

Despite hearing the horse's hooves louder still, and with dozens and dozens of male members of the Almber in full retreat, scattering all over the beach, the heavy beat of her heart in her ears was by far the loudest sound.

"Hurry up!" she said.

The response wasn't the one she expected—the one she'd *hoped* for.

Instead of grabbing hold of her hand, she heard Rut reply to her, with that same leisurely—almost *carefree*—manner from before. "Hildie, don't you see?"

Half occupied by the gloom surrounding the village, wondering from which direction the horses would advance from out of the darkness, and with half her mind on the inanities spewing forth from Rut's mouth, she replied, "See *what*?"

"She came to me too—just now."

Hildie shook her head, turned her attention back down, into the hole. "What're you talking about?" she said. "Just take hold of my hand—*please!*"

Rut held off for another few moments, and then he finally did clasp hold of her hand, interlock his fingers with her own.

Hildie had always believed that Rut looked something like a blond cannonball, but it never seemed so apt of a comparison until this very moment. Almost as soon as he had gripped hold of her hand, she felt as if he might twist her arm right off.

Hildie muttered an enchantment she'd almost forgotten she

knew; one which would give her much greater, brute-force strength. She felt her fire magic frothing in her veins. It was almost as if some enormous burden shifted off her shoulders.

She gritted her teeth and yanked Rut upward.

Up to the side of the hole.

When Hildie was certain that she couldn't take the pressure exerted on her right arm any longer, she found some extra scrap of strength from somewhere, and she channelled it into hauling Rut entirely free of the hole.

"Come on!" she said. "Take hold!"

Hildie could feel the breath squeezing out of her lungs, and the fatigue in her muscles setting in despite the burn of the magic pumping through her veins. She watched on, almost a witness to the strength of her magic as she lifted Rut free of the hole and, with a satisfied, exhausted exhale, he landed on the other side.

When Hildie turned her head to look off back at the village, she saw the first horse break free of the darkness.

A rider with bright-red skin—skin which shimmered slightly in the light from the moon and torches. She thought that she could make out scabs too; all over the Creature's bare flesh.

What caught her attention most of all, though, was the long, lizard-like snout which protruded from the head.

The whole image sent a nauseous shudder through her stomach.

It was a *Creature* of some description, though she couldn't say which.

She had never had much experience with Creatures—nobody throughout Shellacnass had—they'd been outlawed from before when she was born.

If they *had* been present in the kingdom then they had

managed to do so by keeping an extremely low profile. Or by some other means.

On her knees, still reeling from the surge of fire magic through her blood, and the steady, pumping heartbeats at her temples, she looked over the assembled forces of the Almber . . . how the male members had all formed themselves into a long line and how they held their spears upward; in an attempt to pierce the advancing horses right through their soft bellies.

As good a strategy as they might employ.

Her heart rapped against her tonsils as she watched the horse, with the rider perched on top, attempt to leap over the impromptu wall of spears.

The horse's hind legs hardly left the ground before half a dozen spears pierced the underside of its belly; and sent the horse, and rider, tumbling over into the sand.

The horse whinnied and thrashed its hooves, sending up clouds of sand which blew on the calm night-time breeze; away off into the gloom surrounding the village.

The rider, meanwhile, quickly scrabbled to his feet; only to be halted in his escape by an onslaught of spears from the male members of the Almber. Black blood shone dully from between his muscular shoulders.

And the rider's dying *groan* reverberated about Almber's Bay.

Hildie turned her attention back to the darkness outside, to the route which would lead to the plains. She waited. And waited. Knowing that more would be coming.

She felt a flush of confidence; that the Almber would be able to repel this—their *latest* foe. That she wouldn't need to expose her magic. That she wouldn't have to risk being outcast by them . . . just as every other community had made her an outcast.

As Hildie's breathing became deeper and deeper, as she recovered her senses more and more and managed to push down the magical urges fighting for control of her brain, she tried to do her best to convince herself that this was the end; that there would be no more of the invasion. That the invaders—these *Creatures*—had given up before they'd even started.

Their sneak-attack foiled.

But it was then that Hildie caught sight of the silhouettes; the horses all appearing out of the darkness, riders on the back of each.

They were emerging on all sides, having surrounded the village.

She watched on as the Almber shifted the position of their wall of spears. Each time that a new horseman emerged, they tried their best to rotate themselves and rearrange their forces so that they might be able to repel the attack from whichever direction it might come.

Hildie knew that this attack was well organised; that it had—most likely—been long planned. The chances of the Almber seeing off these horsemen without some kind of outside intervention seemed depressingly low.

Hildie turned to look at Rut, who'd she'd almost forgotten about. When she took in his features, she saw that he was blinking rapidly—squeezing his eyes shut and then opening them wide. He rubbed his temples several times.

Hildie shook her head.

This was just what she needed; some bumbling *fool* for company.

And to think that she could've just as easily allowed him to die.

She reminded herself why she hadn't.

The Webbing Armoury.

The three magical artefacts; the Webbing Blade, Bow and Cloak. The weapons which would be the making of a Spider Warrior.

Infused with ice magic.

So, no use for her, in theory . . . but that didn't mean that knowledge of the location of the Webbing Armoury wouldn't grant its own subtle form of power.

And she had made the snap decision, back on the edge of the hole, that she would keep Rut onside for as long as she could stomach.

Until she could ascertain whether or not he was telling the truth.

She turned her attention back to the Creatures; to these *red-skinned* riders.

10

RED-SKINNED RIDERS

A S RUT CROUCHED DOWN beside the hole which'd served as his gaol moments before, he could feel the giddiness leaving him.

It had been a strange sensation, a sort of tingling feeling which'd passed over the entire surface of his skull. It had turned the world bleary, made him feel almost *drunk* . . . and then Hildie had arrived from above him, and she had reached down . . . saved him.

The strength which she had shown to him was almost unbelievable . . . how she had dragged him—someone of *his weight*—up and out of that sandy pit, why, it *almost* defied belief . . . although he did suppose that, in the course of his journey, he had lost a great deal of heft. Still, it had been an extremely worthy feat all the same.

Rut was aware of lots happening all around him.

He could see, across the beach, horsemen . . . *red-skinned horsemen* . . . and then the squat, brown-skinned, indigenous people who'd taken him prisoner.

The horsemen were closing in on the indigenous people, who held out their spears, as if daring the horsemen to attempt to breach the perimeter they had created.

He could see, before them, where the indigenous people had already killed one of the red-skinned horsemen, left him for dead in the sand. Once more, he could smell blood on the air, mixed in with that musky scent of horse. It sent his mind back to the night they had captured him.

His heart raced.

Wasn't that what they had intended for him?

Death.

He felt all the muscles in his body lock tight; then he shifted a glance off in Hildie's direction. He thought about how she seemed almost *at home* here; in this village, with the Almber.

But hadn't that been what the spy reports had said?

That she had become integrated here?

. . . At least that was the information which Lou had passed onto him; what Lou's surveillance network—the Eye—had informed Rut.

And Rut was supposed to be the one to bring Hildie back to the Crystal City.

For what reason, he had no idea.

As he analysed the stalemate playing out before his eyes between the strange red-skinned—*Creatures*?—he thought back to what had happened to him down in the hole; down in that sandy gaol.

He recalled how he had felt all at once impossibly hot and incredibly cold.

It had happened soon after the sun had gone down and the night had moved in.

Like Rut had for most of his stay in the gaol, he had been thinking about his family; about what they might be doing right at that moment. He had thought about the apple orchard his wife Emelda had lovingly sprouted into life; and he thought about his daughter, Forre, skipping between the low-hanging branches in the late-afternoon sunlight. He had almost been able to breathe in the thick scent of the apples; and it had sent a quiver through his entire body to believe that his wife and daughter were on the other side of the kingdom without a care in the world, without even the merest clue that Rut might be in a perilous state.

While Rut had been in the hole, he had believed that he'd kept his eyes shut, but he'd soon realised that his eyes had been very much open; and that what he'd been doing was akin to dreaming while awake.

What had brought him around from his dreaming had been the sight of the figure above him. The glittering, bronze-skinned figure. Reaching their hand down to him.

One of the villagers.

One of the Almber.

He had known that right away.

And yet, he had been taken off guard by the sight, knowing that none of the guards stationed around the circumference of the hole would allow anyone near.

That it must be a mirage, or how ever he could call this delusion.

It had only been when Rut had found his feet that he had noted the sleek, black, shoulder-length hair. And that outstretched hand.

A girl; a young *girl*.

Strangely, Rut had felt an intense happiness rip through him; as if somebody had painlessly cracked open his chest and dosed him with a whole pub's worth of brandy ale; direct to his heart.

He had felt his body wracked with shivering, and he'd reached out for the hand.

Felt his fingertips brush those of the girl.

And then it'd been as if something outside the gaol had startled the girl, because she had withdrawn from the hole, disappeared from sight.

One of the guards had peered in then, brandishing a spear, that mean look of anger sketched all across his face.

And Rut, like a rat, had recoiled back down into the shadows of the hole.

Afraid that the girl might be some message from the gods.

That Rut was soon to depart this world.

But nothing else had happened.

He had simply remained at the bottom of the pit.

Waiting . . . waiting . . . *for Hildie*.

11

A WROUGHT NEGOTIATION

HILDIE WATCHED the Almber facing off with the red-skinned riders.

The horses continued to circle, and the Almber did likewise; matching them movement for movement. As she continued to watch, she noted one of the horsemen take steps toward the Almber's spears. She wondered if these Creatures were lacking in intelligence; if they would simply keep throwing themselves at the Almber's spears until none of them remained.

And not in a single bulk assault; but one at a time.

But the horseman who broke away from the rest of the group —unlike the other one, now deceased—didn't attempt to leap over the top of the spears.

Instead, the horseman dismounted; landing in the sand with his feet spread well apart.

From here, Hildie realised that she could better judge their clothing.

When she had seen them for the first time, she had believed that the horsemen—that these Creatures; if that was what they were—had been naked.

Now, though, she saw that they were only stripped to the waist, and that all the riders wore hardy leather riding trousers.

She wondered to herself if these particular Creatures sweated in the heat because, if they did, they must've been awfully uncomfortable.

Their bodies were all muscular but the dismounted horseman's was *especially* so.

The dismounted horseman took a couple of steps toward the Almber spearmen.

Hildie cast a glance over the Almber's worried faces, from one to the next. As she had learned well from her time here, the Almber didn't have any sort of formally designated leader; and that the cogs of their society just seemed to turn of their own accord; all of them bound together by some common set of beliefs or shared values. She had come to believe that it was a truly beautiful thing and—many times at night—had smirked herself to sleep thinking about how any similar system would be completely impracticable in Ilsnare; the so-called Crystal City.

The citizens of Ilsnare's manners certainly *weren't* by any measure 'Crystal'.

She expected one of the Almber to break ranks and to rush the dismounted horseman—and then for a whole band of other male Almber to join in—but she realised that the Almber were exercising patience.

They weren't leaping into any sort of irrational action.

Despite the fact that no leaders existed among their community, it wasn't to say that decisions weren't reached in a logical fashion.

The understanding between them all was so clear and so well defined that—quite simply—there was no need for words.

Hildie's whole body quivered and she felt the bite of fire magic in her stomach.

She knew that the deep, powerful forces in her were ready.

And that they anticipated an outpouring.

All she had to do was let *go* . . . if she wanted to save the Almber.

The dismounted horseman took another few steps forward so that he now stood with his cheek almost touching the edge of one of the spears.

Hildie felt the blood well in her veins.

She knew that it'd only take one careless gesture.

One swift *stab* . . . and it would cut the horseman open.

Something, at the back of her mind, willed the action.

She wondered if her magic didn't try to *reach out* . . . to influence proceedings.

But Hildie could control such urges.

She wasn't some adolescent mage any longer.

As the dismounted horseman stood facing the line of Almber, she felt a biting chill enter the air, and she wondered if it might be winter just around the corner . . . winter in the tropics; she would never have been able to imagine such a thing.

It was then that Hildie felt her breath being taken away.

The dismounted horseman, this red-skinned *Creature*, began to speak in the Almber's tongue. To—fluently, at least to Hildie's ear—reel through whatever it was he had to tell them . . . the truth was that the dismounted horseman spoke so quickly that Hildie found it almost impossible to follow the thread of what he was saying.

She shifted a glance at Rut and was glad to see that he now wore a more sombre expression; that whatever exhilaration had dominated his features moments before had disappeared. She didn't know just how long she would've been able to handle him if he had kept up that same spirit from before; especially while she was attempting to pay attention to this conversation between the dismounted horseman and the Almber.

As Hildie watched over the proceedings, she caught the whiff of something on the air.

An oily, fishy smell.

What she supposed to be the scent of these Creatures.

It was then that Rut decided to speak up, and Hildie almost throttled him to death for doing so, such was her concentration.

"Horrox," Rut said, his voice—*thankfully*—at the level of a whisper.

Hildie glanced back at him, still feeling a great deal of annoyance that he couldn't just keep his mouth shut. "What?" she said, keeping her voice down too.

"Shape shifters," Rut continued, "they've always lived among us . . . only now they've decided to begin to show themselves."

Hildie felt wrinkles form in her brow.

She turned back to the interaction between the Almber and the 'Horrox' . . . these red-skinned Creatures.

Although she would've hated to admit it out loud, she was glad that she could finally pin some sort of name onto them.

The red-skinned Creature—the *Horrox*—continued to speak with the Almber using their own language. Hildie had to admit to herself that she felt a twinge of envy. Although she had spent the best part of a year in their company, she wasn't anywhere near attaining the grasp of the language this Horrox possessed.

But she did manage to pick out the odd word.

And she could just about tell from the gestures of the Horrox —eerily similar to those which the Almber themselves performed —that the subject had to do with the golden dust embedded in the sand of Almber's Bay.

She had supposed that to be at the source of the Almber's aggression to strangers.

Although Hildie wasn't interested herself, she supposed that all sorts of potions—all sorts of *commerce*—could be made possible from its harvesting.

And whether the Almber defended their bay so valiantly because they realised the dust's true worth—and its possible abuses—or because of simply wanting to keep their territory their own, made no difference.

She noted the Horrox backtracking, explaining himself again and again; going over the same points as if the Almber might not be understanding the whole picture here . . . everything which they were detailing out for them.

After several of these iterations, Hildie finally grasped that the Horrox was attempting to make it understood that he wished to purchase a certain unspecified amount of the golden dust which was located between the grains of sand of the bay. And she also gauged the growing frustration in the Horrox's voice as the Almber didn't so much as raise a word in response; not even to denigrate the Horrox's attempts at an exchange.

But Hildie knew the truth.

That what the Horrox proposed was simply beyond the comprehension of the Almber.

Why would they want to trade their golden dust?

What could *possibly* be in the deal for them?

Already, from the small amount which Rut had told her about the Horrox, she could see what the blockage was in the negotiations.

The Horrox lived among Mortal societies.

And so, how could they possibly understand the Almber?

Hildie wished that she might be able to break her cover, that she might be able to straighten herself up and speak with the Horrox . . . but she knew it would be a risky move and one which could well set off a conflict.

Something which had to be avoided at all costs.

Because, she was certain, these Creatures would easily be able to crush the Almber.

. . . Unless they had a *fire mage* by their side . . .

She watched on as the Horrox continued to attempt an explanation. She noticed how he swung his arms in a more violent fashion in the direction of the sand at their feet—perhaps a gesture which the Horrox might've hardly noticed himself; but Hildie could already note the effect it had on the Almber . . . all of them standing side by side with their spears sticking up in the air; some of them pointed at the Horrox himself.

Everything happened slowly—and yet, at the same time, impossibly fast.

Hildie both had time to think that she could *do* something . . . and to realise that it had already happened.

The Almber, irritated by the violent gesture of the Horrox, as one ploughed forward and buried their spearheads in the Creature's throat.

12
———

MELEE

HILDIE FELT HERSELF frozen in time as she observed the
spearheads cut through the Horrox's skin; bringing that
same black blood welling to the surface. The oily, fishy scent grew
thicker in the air and Hildie felt it right down to her gut. She could
feel the magic brewing through her bloodstream and her heart
tap-tapping against the soft underside of her throat.

The Horrox dropped down to his knees, and then fell onto
his side.

Just like the first one had.

Dead.

Another one.

Dead.

Hildie hardly had time to look around, to see that Rut was up on
his feet, and rushing toward the Almber; when a piercing *shriek*
filled the air . . . what she later processed to be the Horrox's battle cry.

She felt it reverberate in her eardrums and tingle its way down her spine.

Something about the shriek was unnatural.

And it shook her deeply.

Before she had time to think, she felt her feet acting.

They propelled her along, in Rut's slipstream.

Her eyes remained locked on the face-off.

As the Horrox—on horseback—rushed the Almber.

She tried to keep track of Rut's progress at the same time as the battle playing out beyond; and she felt her heart squeezing tight in her chest before—*mercifully*—retracting once again.

Already, silver light from the hexes flung through the air; downing the Almber.

The brown-skinned indigenous people who'd taken Hildie in as one of their own dying grasping their throats as invisible hands strangled them.

Hildie felt her fire magic steaming harder through her veins.

And she knew that she could do something.

That she *had* to do something.

Fast.

She called out to Rut, but he couldn't hear her over the Horrox's battle cry; and he continued on his way.

Where he was headed—escaping into the darkness?—she had no idea.

But she knew that she couldn't go with him.

That would be *too* terrible.

It was as if she'd cast killing curses only yesterday as she snapped her wrists, flinging them through the air at the Horrox. She watched on as several of her curses caught their targets. And observed the Horrox tumbling off the backs of their horses, falling stone dead into the sands.

She supposed that none of the Horrox had bargained on getting themselves involved in a magical battle; otherwise they might've had the good sense to cast a protective charm about their group . . . they had believed that it would be a simple matter of reasoning with the savages that were the Almber; *stampeding* them if the Horrox failed to get their way.

Even as Hildie fired off yet more curses at the invading enemies—at the Horrox—she felt a chill filling her from inside; even though flames roared within her chest.

She hated to recall Mortals.

And how they lived.

This notion—this notion of *war*—it all came from them.

Hildie had killed ten or eleven Horrox before they recognised where she was located, and turned their attention away from slaughtering the Almber armed only with spears, and onto her.

Already, Hildie could tell that their numbers were too many; that she would have no chance of taking them all on . . . she needed another three, perhaps four, mages to have a chance. Although her father—Ma'reygar—had versed her well in magical combat, and they had spoken about Creatures, it had been a far more academic part of his teachings.

Because it had been believed that the Creatures had long ago been banished to the darkened nooks and crannies of the Sable Mountains; or else chased into the neighbouring kingdom; into Rozark.

But, as Hildie had come to learn throughout her life, the education which she had been provided as a child—the education which her father had provided—didn't always prove to be infallible when tested by the real world . . . just as it was being tested now.

Even with the Horrox advancing on her, she thought about how it had required physical blows to be struck before she had been able to break free of her childhood training; and as she did think of it, she felt another smirk form on her lips.

If she was going to die right now, then it would be appropriate.

A far more appropriate death than *she* deserved.

13

FLEEING

RUT PUMPED HIS LEGS harder still, and he was glad that he had lost a great deal of his previous 'jolly' mass.

It was surprising to him just how easily he could move now that much of his fat had been lost on the journey here. And how he didn't get tired as he would before . . . sometimes from simply standing up to get out of his chair; or helping himself down off the back of his horse.

He felt the sweat streak down the sides of his face; and he could feel a great heat growing behind him. He caught the strange scent of fish in his nostrils . . . not that vibrant—*fresh*—salty odour which he had grown accustomed to smelling in the markets he'd passed by on his way here; more like the night-time, hand-drawn wooden carts he would see clacking over the cobblestones of the villages; the cart stacked to bursting with the day's refuse.

In his mouth, Rut could still feel the sand.

In his ears, the *shriek* of the Horrox continued to reverberate.

The idea of who the Creatures were had come to him soon after he'd gathered his thoughts back together and—judging by Hildie's reaction—it was information which she hadn't previously known. At least he had been good for *something* . . .

He put all else out of his mind . . . he put it behind him.

In his wake.

Because, up ahead, he could still see her.

Slipping away into the darkness.

The young, indigenous—Almber girl.

Her skin glistening with gold in the moonlight.

The same girl who had come to him in the sand gaol; and offered him a helping hand.

She had beckoned him away—*away* from the melee.

Although Rut had once been a skuller—one of those who had defended the plains of the Northern Villages from the crazed, cursed animals which appeared at night—he would be the first to admit that he had never been all that handy with a sword . . . or, really, any sort of weapon; his spear-handling—certainly—wasn't what he might count as a strength.

The truth of it was that working as a skuller had been good money; and for the few times he'd found himself tangled in some fight or other; it had been worthwhile.

That was until everything had up and changed.

Until the village where he'd grown up, Quagsmile, had been burned down.

Burned down by Hildie.

Rut pushed himself harder and harder, feeling his muscles draw tighter with every stride.

He was afraid that he might stumble—*trip*—and that he would break a limb doing so.

That really *would* be the end . . . once the Horrox had done with the Almber they would scour the periphery and they would come across him.

They would *kill* him.

He was nothing to them.

If only they knew that he possessed the secret to the location of the Webbing Armoury.

Well, *half* of it, at least.

As Rut buried himself deeper and deeper in the darkness, keeping his eyes glued to the figure of the girl up ahead, he heard yet more shrieks. He felt more heat on the side of his face. He knew that Hildie was casting spells, that she was working her fire magic.

Her travels hadn't inhibited the efficacy of her powers, it seemed.

The girl led him over the sandy, grassy earth which surrounded the bay, and several times Rut felt his foot sink into a hole—made by a rabbit or some other vermin. When he thought that he'd almost lost sight of her, he realised that she was just up ahead.

That she was now standing still.

He felt the irradiating glow emanating out from her.

That strange, ethereal warmth which ebbed through the air.

Which brought sweat seeping out of his skin.

He looked to her lips, expecting her to speak to him, for her to tell him where to hide. But when she did speak to him, it wasn't through her lips.

It was directly into his mind.

— *Wait here.*

Rut felt his mind throb within his skull.

His heart kicked on another few beats.

He just about managed to vocalise the beginning of a sentence, "What . . ." but she was too quick for him, and her voice echoed about his mind once again.

— *Do not trust her. Your anger is well placed. When the time is right, you must run.*

And, with that, Rut observed her disappear into the darkness. *Gone.*

14

MAGICAL RAMPAGE

HILDIE FELT THE ENTIRE WORLD burst into flames. All around her.

It had been too much . . . *far* too much for her to control.

Even as she felt the fireball consuming her, her heart surely throbbing faster than she ever thought might be possible, she knew that her magic had been welled up within her; just waiting for its opportunity to burst forth and make its mark on the world.

And now it had.

She saw nothing for the flames which lapped on all sides; a sea of fire.

In the burning blaze, she could make out the vague silhouettes of the Horrox; those who hadn't escaped from her influence before she had unleashed everything she had.

Her entire mind was occupied with fire, and she could see nothing else; she could *think* nothing else. Nothing but the flow of magic, up through her body, and then out through her chest.

From her fingertips.

If only her father—Ma'reygar—had been here.

He would've been *so* proud.

All this time, all of the will power Hildie had exercised.

She had so badly wanted to control her magic.

She had wanted to be able to manage it.

To make it dance to her own tune.

But, in the end, she had simply been unable.

'Walking with weakness' could only help her so far . . .

Perhaps her fire magic would've flowed free from her veins for the rest of time if it hadn't been for her Mortal body's complaints. She could feel the fatigue, growing out of her mind, and then stretching itself down over her muscles; consuming the rest of her body.

At first the blaze which sprouted from her fingertips waned.

And then she felt the heat of the fire weaken.

Other senses returned to her.

She could smell that rotten odour of fish.

And she could hear the gentle *sweep* of the sea washing in against the sandy shore.

The wall of fire retreated.

A cooling breeze blew in from the sea.

Hildie thought that she heard the distant *cackle* of a seagull.

Then, the moonlight seeming to hush the dying flames, Hildie picked out the figures scattered around her on all sides. They lay so still, in the sand, their forms nothing more than lifeless sacks.

The Horrox all slayed . . .

As she took stock of them, as her eyes lingered over their scattered bodies, she noted that they had been fleeing her. That they were all lying on their fronts; their plan of escape thwarted. Their horses, too, were reduced to nothing but barbecued hides.

She hadn't been able to pull back her magic . . . that was what she told herself, anyway . . . she tried not to allow the notion that something in her Mortal soul might've *enjoyed* dragging them back to her—*killing them all.*

She had satisfied her fire magic.

And, despite the many dead collected around her, she felt fulfilled for the first time in *such* a long while.

Why had she been searching for so long when *this* was the feeling she sought?

But it was then, with the sensation of a long-suffered hunger vanquished, that she turned her attention to the village further back on the beach; to the Almber.

Their huts . . . the hut they had built for her . . . all of them smouldered away—some with the embers continuing to glow out of their wreckage.

She looked to the male members of the Almber; they, too, just as with the Horrox, had been scorched into cinders by Hildie's outpouring of magic.

It was then that Hildie felt as if a chilling blade had been slipped into her ribcage, directly into her heart.

And she knew just who she was.

That whatever fleeting feeling of satisfaction she might have taken from the outpouring of magic, the ravished bodies of the Almber lying all around overwhelmed it completely.

It was the same again . . . she had allowed her selfish nature to get in the way.

She had *had* to be the hero.

The one to save them all.

And, in so doing, she had destroyed all that was good.

Hildie felt the chill within her body increase and she began to shiver.

Her teeth chattered.

She tasted the enamel, and a little blood.

She realised that—during her magical rampage—she must've bitten into her tongue; something within her Mortal body imploring her to stop . . . to prevent the fire magic which ran through her blood from coming to bear on the outside world; on her exterior body.

As Hildie walked through the remains of the village—the remains of Almber's Bay—she looked to the charred bodies, beneath the huts.

Those wooden structures had only acted as ovens, pinning the victims beneath.

She could see where the sand had turned to glass from the intense heat.

Where it had become transparent; and *golden* . . . almost as if it was stained glass, like she might have observed back at Ravens-bark; the monastery which'd been destroyed in her father's magical war over a decade earlier.

Not knowing what she should do now, she turned away from the dead villagers and headed off into the gloom which surrounded the beach. She knew that, by first light, the scavengers would have arrived—not just the predatory animals which lived on the grassy plains which surrounded the beach; but the humans too.

At last, Mortals would be able to lay their hands on the prized golden dust.

She hoped they would be satisfied.

As Hildie took her final steps away from the village, she spotted some movement; among the splinters, charred wood; and the sand transformed into shards of golden glass.

Nothing more than a shape.

A silhouette . . . just as the Horrox had appeared to her while they'd been trapped within her firestorm.

Hildie stood still and stared.

In wonder.

How could *anybody* possibly survive this?

How could *anyone* have lived?

. . . A miracle.

Something—*somebody*—who had lived through her ire.

Hildie trod closer.

Closer still.

And then she stood over the person.

A girl.

Her skin still glittering with the golden dust.

She looked . . . *familiar* . . . somehow.

15

LEAVING ALMBER'S BAY

HILDIE FELT THE WARMTH of the late-morning sun up against her neck.

She felt its rays brush against her skin.

Make the fire magic in her veins *hum.*

Her feet felt heavy and her entire body was wracked with fatigue.

Hildie felt the girl's dainty fingers wrapped about her own as they trudged over the stodgy plains which surrounded Almber's Bay. When she'd asked the girl her name, she had remained silent, as if afraid of her. And she hadn't pursued the matter. She supposed that the girl was still traumatised from the experience of the night before.

And why wouldn't she be?

Everything she'd known—every*one* she'd known—was gone.

Hildie felt the long grasses of the plains brushing up against her bare calves.

She hadn't had a chance to change out of her dress before the attack had come about.

When she tilted her head upward, she saw that Rut was striding several paces ahead. He had on the same undershirt that the Almber had brought him to the village in; as their prisoner. It seemed that he, more than Hildie or the little Almber girl—the last of her kind—was the most anxious to put as much distance between himself and Almber's Bay as physically possible.

They hadn't returned to gaze over the scattered bodies.

To wonder at Hildie's power.

The girl, like the other villagers, wore raggedy clothing; a sort of cloth tunic which Hildie supposed had once been a brown colour. But the sun and rain had turned it more of a grey-green shade. The child still had a girlish skip to her gait and, unaccustomed to being around children as Hildie was, she kept expecting her to take a tumble . . . to end up lying on her back and staring up at the sky.

But the girl, like the rest of the Almber, knew these plains well.

She knew this unsteady ground well.

As the girl skipped along beside her, Hildie couldn't help but notice Rut had come to a halt; a little way ahead of them.

Hildie glanced down to the little girl, somehow realising that this was something which should be kept away from her eyes . . . especially after what she had witnessed the night before; some vain attempt to ward off the creeping realisation that the girl was in the company of nothing less than a living, breathing monster.

In a Mortal body.

"Wait here," Hildie said to the girl, in the Almber tongue.

The girl nodded in reply, and Hildie left her where she stood, glancing back over her shoulder several times to make sure that she hadn't deigned to follow in that mischievous way which all children had a habit of doing.

Hildie approached Rut.

She moved through the long grasses, still hearing the wash of the tide on the beach; the *cackle* of gulls in the air. Nature seemed so oblivious; so indifferent. As if nothing at all had happened the night before.

And yet, Hildie knew that she would miss living on the beach so much . . . she would miss Almber's Bay *so much* . . . it was difficult to tell herself that it no longer existed.

And that *she* had been the one to destroy it.

It was as if somebody had severed one of her legs then told her to keep on walking.

But, then again, she reminded herself—turning her attention downward to the stump, all that remained of her left hand—that she had lost limbs before. And although it was painful, she had to keep moving on; any other option was inconceivable.

She couldn't give up.

Not with fire magic in her veins.

Not with the power which dwelled within her.

Once she had been so convinced she could do good.

Perhaps she still might be able.

Had everything—*her life*—simply been a matter of misfortune?

Being in the wrong place at the wrong time?

As Hildie drew up to Rut's shoulder, she was struck by the rancid stench.

She knew the smell well.

She had grown to recognise it instantly on her travels.

Rotting horse meat.

Often, while she would be walking along a countryside road, she would catch that smell in her nostrils and, without fail, she would come across a horse's carcass dumped into the long grasses; left to decompose. From the horses which Hildie had come across, most of them had been cart horses. She supposed, with a slightly grim edge to her thoughts, that since most carts were drawn by various horses the ones which outright collapsed could be safely discarded.

It all sounded so ... *human.*

She listened to the buzz of flies; watched on as their tiny, black bodies weaved about the horse's carcass. This was the horse which Rut had travelled here on ... the one which the Almber had —*apparently*—slaughtered when they'd captured him.

Sometimes Hildie found herself contemplating such things, wondering how such a peaceable people could suddenly turn so savage; almost in the flutter of an eyelash.

Then again, she supposed that the horse, to them, represented an escape—another life—a way of leaving Almber's Bay forever.

And nobody ever left Almber's Bay.

Not really.

Not even Hildie, Rut, and the little girl.

A part of them *would* remain there forever whatever happened.

Hildie half expected Rut to break down into tears at the sight of the horse, lying there in the long grasses. She saw that there was a leather bedroll lying on the ground. It seemed as though the Almber had caught Rut soon after he'd bedded down for the night.

The Almber would always attack at night, whenever it was possible. Since they knew the terrain far better than any invader, they could take prisoners by using the element of surprise against them.

Rut never would've had a chance to defend himself.

Easy-pickings for the Almber.

As Hildie stood at Rut's shoulder, saw the way that he fixed his stare down on the dead horse, she had the urge to reach out and touch him.

Her good right hand shook as she stretched out and, carefully, laid her hand on his shoulder. She noted him flinch slightly at her touch but, otherwise, he didn't react.

He continued to stare down at his horse.

Finally Hildie broke the silence. "Shall we go?" she said.

Rut continued to stare down at the horse, lying there in the grasses, and then, as if he had been in the throes of some distant dream, he blinked away the delusion before his nose and turned to her.

He gave her a sturdy nod.

And they went on their way.

16

A VILLAGE

SEVERAL TIMES, Hildie wanted to question the direction in which Rut was leading them. Soon after they'd left the horse's carcass behind, he had informed them that he knew the way to the closest village. When he'd informed Hildie that it was a day's ride away she had felt her gut dip.

The reality that they had left behind Almber's Bay without taking so much as a flask of water, or a hunk of fish or pork with them, hit home.

Hildie, though, found that she was more concerned for the welfare of the little girl.

She didn't want her to experience any sort of discomfort.

She had no one now . . . no one except for herself and Rut.

As Hildie trudged on across the grassy plains, she felt that realisation dawn on her; that there was nowhere for the little girl to go. That she was now entrusted to Rut and Hildie's care. Hildie had never wanted to be a mother; had never wanted any close family of her own . . . because, in her childhood, family had only brought her pain.

Did that matter now?

Hildie was certain that she could work it out later—that she and *Rut* could work it out later.

The first thing which grabbed Hildie's attention about their route from Almber's Bay was that Rut had claimed that they would need to pass through a forest on their way to the village. But, even as the sun began to set—the flaming-hot sun setting over the horizon, and her fire magic dwindling to embers—she couldn't make out so much as a single tree.

In the twilight, she could, however, make out a tiny settlement; half a dozen houses all scattered about on the sandy plains which surrounded the coastline.

When she looked to Rut to see if this was the village he had intended them to arrive at, he gave her a vacant smile and she supposed that this was just a happy accident.

Still, all the same, she was glad for it.

The houses in the village were poorly built; made from cheap, wooden off-cuts. Hildie could smell the mildew in the air from where the humid conditions of the tropics had begun to rot the wood. There were countless small settlements like this, scattered all about this area of the kingdom; but Hildie had also come to understand that they were valuable.

That they could often be a useful source for water or food.

Both of which they desperately needed right now.

The road through the village was nothing more than worn-down sand; but worn down by the soles of shoes, or boots, not by horses' hooves.

Hildie felt a quiver pass up her spine.

She knew that the population of a backwater village such as this one would most likely be extremely suspicious about strangers.

Just as the Almber had been.

When Hildie looked about the village, she noted that it was deserted. That nobody looked out through their doors to see them approaching. She noted that several of the front doors were left wide open.

Then again, she supposed that there was little need for the villagers to lock their doors here. By necessity they would need to trust their neighbours.

Anything that went missing would be attributed to strangers.

Strangers like herself, Rut and the little girl.

Noticing the little girl lagging on her heels, Hildie stopped, turned to her and called her close.

When she took hold of the little girl's hand, she squeezed it tightly.

Hildie's eyes danced about the village, keeping a lookout for any of the inhabitants.

Still, though, nobody to see.

"Over here!" Rut called out from ahead.

The sound of Rut's voice sent a shimmer through Hildie's bones.

It cut through the near-silent air, disturbed only by the faint sea breeze.

More than anything else, Hildie wanted to tell Rut to be quiet.

She wanted him to shut his mouth.

And yet, at the same time, she saw where he indicated.

A well.

Made of stone.

Small.

Its opening was large enough only for the quarter-gallon wooden bucket on the end of the frayed rope. But it was a start.

Hildie watched on as Rut approached the well.

At any second, she was expecting a net, propelled by some sort of hidden mechanism, to appear from beneath the well; and for Rut to fly upward, tangled-up, and unable to do anything to prevent his upward motion; and his capture.

His second capture in as many days.

What was it they said about foolishness and misfortune?

... That the two often went together.

Hildie hung back, holding the little girl from going forward.

Before Hildie could put any of her fears into words, it was too late.

Rut had grabbed hold of the wooden bucket and tossed it into the well. He maneuvered the bucket within the structure using the rope which hung down from the bracket above. He peered down into the hole, squinting, apparently having trouble making out just what he might be doing down there in the dimming light.

Although Hildie would've liked them to leave this village behind—for them to carry on with their journey away from Almber's Bay—she also knew that her entire body craved water; and that the little girl, too, craved water.

Without it—without at least a *cup*—they might not make it through the next day.

Rut brought the wooden bucket up from the well, and then, rivulets of water overflowing the sides—clear, *fresh*, water—he looked back over his shoulder and smiled at them. "Come on," he said. "Ladies drink first."

Hildie put the sentiment out of her mind.

She often found herself rolling her eyes, or smirking at such *base* remarks from men; with the implication that they were stronger than the 'fairer sex'.

Well, from her own—*personal*—experience, she noted that men bled just as easily as women and children. And they certainly *died* just as easily.

Hildie trod forward, feeling the dryness at the back of her throat as an almost uncontrollable urge now. She kept the little girl close to her side, too, not wanting her to go wandering off into one of the houses . . . to come across one of the residents.

Hildie couldn't face anyone else dying because of her neglect.

Because she couldn't *control* herself.

When Hildie got to the well, she reached for the bucketful of water and then handed it down to the little girl.

The little girl took the bucket in her two hands, exercising great concentration in trying not to spill it. Slowly, she brought the rim of the bucket up to her lips. She slurped at the water within, taking it in her mouth.

Hildie watched as the little girl's throat bobbed with her swallows.

Everything about the little girl's actions seemed to strike her in the gut—it affected her on a deep emotional level.

She wondered if it was because she had never had children.

But that she still had the motherly urge.

Buried deep within her.

When the little girl got through with drinking, Rut took the bucket and tossed it back down into the well. As he brought it back up again, Hildie wondered if she would be able to control herself. Her entire body now seemed wracked with thirst. Her hands shook as she tightened her grip about the sides of the bucket and then brought the water to her lips.

Several drops trickled down her chin and splashed onto the front of her dress.

But the chilly, damp sensation against her skin seemed only to propel her urge . . . to stoke her thirst all the more.

Before she knew it, she'd tipped back the entire contents of the bucket and felt the water swilling about her belly.

She glanced back at Rut, and saw that he was grinning from ear to ear.

More than anything else, she remarked at the fact that he managed to put on so much as a smile considering that he must be suffering from his own personal thirst.

Hildie could feel her entire body shaking as she watched Rut drop the bucket down the well for a third time. When he brought it up again, she had the urge to rip it from his hands and to drink the contents for herself.

But she restrained herself.

She wasn't alone anymore.

She wasn't in *lone-survival* mode anymore.

And yet, that was a difficult mind-set to free herself from.

She knew that it would take her days before she felt entirely comfortable in the company of the little girl and Rut . . . before she managed to get her head around the fact that she had more than her own skin to protect.

Why, if what Rut had said was true, that he held the key to the Webbing Armoury, then it might well be that the entirety of the kingdom depended on her for its safety.

The reason that decision had been made, the reason that Lou .

. . *King* Louson of Shellacnass . . . had made that decision; still rankled with her.

Even now, watching Rut drink from the bucket, some of the water trickling down his chin, just as it had when she had drunk, she couldn't quite believe that he had managed to survive such a journey all on his own.

Perhaps he'd had more help than he'd let on . . . or, at the very least, more company than that deceased horse of his.

Rut finally finished up his drinking and dumped the bucket back into the well.

Hildie heard a dampened splash from within.

Rut nodded to the village. "I'm going to check the place out," he said. "See if it's safe for us to stay here tonight."

Hildie felt another quiver pass through her.

Even without any knowledge of this village; without her having so much as set foot over the threshold of one of these homes, she sensed something profoundly disquieting about the whole place. And she wished to get away from here just as soon as was practicably possible.

Hildie helped the little girl to another few bucketfuls of water, until—*apparently satisfied*—she skittered away and went off chasing the moths which fluttered about the long grasses. Hildie was glad that she was able to take some more water for herself.

Her thirst was deeper than she'd imagined.

She'd just brought up her third bucket of water from the well when she noticed Rut emerging from one of the homes.

The darkness had moved in several minutes before, and the moonlight was all that illuminated the village. There was nobody in the village to light torches.

Even in the scraps of light, she could tell that his complexion was pale.

That his eyes seemed almost black in this light.

He met her gaze.

Stared at her long and hard.

"Dead," he said, his voice quiet, but carrying through the silent village. "They're all dead."

17

THE NEVER-ENDING ECHO

RUT SAT UP STRAIGHT. His back pressed against the sand dunes they'd decided to bed down on for the night. They'd chosen a spot about five minutes away from the village and slightly elevated. It was close enough so that they could double back to the well when the morning light arrived, but far enough so as to give peace of mind.

All those bodies.

Rut could still see them, in his mind's eye.

First it had been the smell—how hadn't he noticed the *smell* before?—that putrid, blood-curdling stench of rotting. It had been almost like a punch to the solar plexus; knocking him backward several steps.

But he had managed to stand firm.

To ignore the bite of bile at the back of his throat.

The sight had brought to mind so many things; so many horrific memories he'd imagined long-ago suppressed.

Back when he'd been a skuller—back when Hildie had burned down the villages, among them his own—he had had to scour through the wreckage looking for anything the survivors might be able to put to use.

There had been hardly anything.

Only the charred remains of bodies.

And the smell hadn't been anything like what he had experienced in those homes; back in that village.

What had most struck him about the bodies he'd seen in the burned-out wreckage of those villages of ashes was the way that they'd all been curled up . . . some of them—*families*—bundled into one another's arms as they awaited their certain fate.

He recalled, back when he had been a child, perhaps seven or eight summers old, he had used to play a game with the other children his age.

At night, often on days of festivity, with their parents incapacitated either from liquor or exhaustion, they would all scatter into the forest outside Quagsmile and, each of them with a purloined torch in their hand to light their way; they would search for ant hills.

Almost always, the ant hills would be located beneath rotten boughs, in the fertile soil created by age and decay. When one of them located an ant hill, it would be that child's responsibility to crouch down beneath the bough and set fire to it; with the aid of a few dried leaves.

They would all, then, stand around the ant hill, each of them bent over, with their hands on their knees, and watch as the ants burned to death.

Rut could still hear the cruel laughter from the children—

laughter which he had joined in with, but, even at the time, felt uncomfortable about.

But he *had* laughed along.

Rut recalled very clearly the day when he'd decided no longer to tag along with the rest of the children. It had been the day that he himself had discovered one of the ant hills.

He could still feel the ripple of excitement passing through his blood, to think that *he* had been the one to locate what would be the centrepiece of their entertainment.

Just as the other children had always done before—just as Rut had *seen* the other children do before—he knelt down on the soft, dead leaves and the slightly damp earth. Then he had reached out and set his torch's flame beneath the ant hill.

He had felt the excited chatter of the children surrounding him, and felt his heart beating hard in his chest, bouncing back against his ribs.

He could still remember the sick smile which'd curled his lips as he had seen the first of those ants—those *animals*—burning to a crisp.

And yet he had hardly *seen* them.

Finally, though, with the giddy laughter of the other children in his ears, he had focussed in on the ant hill and absorbed the sight of the ants properly for the first time.

Maybe he had believed that it was important to know their pain.

Or perhaps he had thought the enjoyment—the *real* enjoyment—the other children found in the spectacle would make itself apparent.

And it was then that he had realised that the ants were not dying in a random fashion.

They didn't scatter about the ant hill; their animal brains on overdrive, desperate to avoid death.

No, they huddled together.

In pairs.

Embracing one another.

It was only now, as Rut leaned against the sand dune, feeling the long grasses tickling the back of his exposed neck, that he wondered if what had befallen him had been some sort of justice exacted on behalf of the gods.

Who was *he*—a human—to believe that he was above animals?

Or Creatures?

Didn't they feel pain like he did?

Didn't they suffer and fear dying alone?

The sight of the homes here, of seeing those corpses in the village; it had brought all of those images back to him. A sort of never-ending echo about his skull.

Rut felt a faint breeze coming in from the sea, mercifully blowing down onto the village, so that it wouldn't waft the *smell* up to where they had bedded down for the night.

He turned his attention to Hildie and the little girl.

He still hadn't found out the little girl's name.

There hadn't seemed to be time.

They had walked for the entirety of the day, until they had reached the village here.

Although he had been so sure that this had been the right way for them to go—the way which would lead to the forest, and then to the village—he now realised that he must've been mistaken.

The landscape was so flat and featureless that it was a sure thing that he would've noticed a village such as this one. He would've wasted no time in stopping by with his horse so that the two of them might get fed and watered.

Rut watched on as the little girl lay in Hildie's arms. Both of them slept with faint smiles clinging to their lips. Neither of them would die alone; and neither would he.

Because they would remain together.

Until they found their way home.

18

PROGRESS

HILDIE COULD HARDLY BELIEVE the progress they made the next day.

Or how mistaken she had been to believe that she'd been situated in the middle of nowhere; with the Almber. Perhaps she'd just wanted to believe that.

Once they'd risen early—at first light—Rut had acted the gentleman and gone off to fetch them water from the village.

When he'd returned, he'd been bearing a flask for each of them. Hildie didn't press him for details on where he had obtained the flasks; she knew that the only plausible explanation was that he had entered one of the many homes and scavenged about until he had found them.

But she was glad that he had done so.

As night had begun to fall, each of them had long ago drained the contents of their flask. But then they'd noticed, almost like a sign from the gods, the gentle orange glow of torchlight on the horizon. They had trodden their way across the sandy plains and, eventually, they'd arrived here: another—much larger—village.

A town, really.

When Hildie had looked to Rut, she had noted the look of surprise—and delight—sketched across his features. And she knew, even without asking, that this most certainly *wasn't* the town where Rut had been leading them.

But, by hook or by crook, he had led them back to civilisation.

The main road which ran through the town had well-tended cobblestones, and several flower baskets hung down from the window boxes above their heads. There was a sense of busyness about the town despite the in-coming night-time.

Torches lit up the streets, soothing the fire in Hildie's veins.

The *clickety-clack* of wheels of horse-drawn carts constantly bounced back off the walls of the houses. Street children, surely up well past their bedtime, in nothing more substantial than soiled rags, rushed about their feet; appearing on all sides.

If Hildie had had anything on her of value, she would've been wary for the feel of the street children's delicate hands.

She noted how the little girl hid herself behind her back while snatching glances at the street children; almost as if she longed to join them but was struck into inaction by the knowledge that her shyness would get the better of her.

Hildie almost had the urge to give the girl a little nudge in the back, so that she might skip off and go play. But the little girl continued to grip tightly to the back of Hildie's dress.

They walked among the townspeople who, despite not wearing the latest fashions, were well-kempt in their appearance. The townspeople smiled politely at the visitors, even though they were obviously foreigners. And each one of them in extreme need of a wash and change of clothes.

At first, Hildie found the constant chatter which rose up into the air all around the town to be almost overwhelming.

When she'd been out on her own, she'd been used to her own company.

And then, when she'd lived with the Almber, she'd become accustomed to their near-silent society.

To suddenly be presented with this bleary soundscape sent a shudder through her stomach, and her fire magic defensively flared through her veins despite the gentle caress of the torchlight.

Just as had happened before she'd struck down the Horrox, she felt the itchy sensation on the tips of her fingers. Her magic wanting to escape the surface of her skin; to be brought to bear on the world so that all might observe her strength.

But she held in the urge.

Just as she knew she must.

Control.

. . . Only control.

Next, there were the delicious odours: freshly picked oranges, apples, the unmistakeable scent of honey ale being brewed . . . and although Hildie had always made it something of an objective of hers to steer clear of alcoholic beverages, she couldn't help but fantasise for a few moments about the warmth which could flood her veins if she so wished.

Almost like magic.

Hildie observed Rut up ahead, and saw that a man wearing a smart navy-blue tunic over a pair of well-pressed, lemon grass-coloured trousers, had approached him.

Like the other inhabitants of this town, the man's appearance was impeccable.

His hair was combed into a side-parting and his skin seemed to gleam in the torchlight which illuminated the town streets.

From what Hildie could overhear, she learned that the man was offering them a room for the night; in one of the taverns across town.

She listened to the man's pitch, finding herself a little lost at times as she found his regional accent almost overbearing. But— just as she had got a handle on the Almber language—she began to get the hang of the man's speech.

Rut simply nodded along with everything the man was saying, and Hildie was somewhat taken by surprise that, when the man offered his hand to Rut, Rut took it from him and shook.

As if they'd agreed a deal.

Before Hildie had a chance to register any objection she might have had to this arrangement, the man grinned at Rut and then disappeared off among the crowds.

Hildie quickened her pace and arrived at Rut's side, with the little girl still clinging to the back of her dress. "What did you agree to?" she said.

Rut stared back at her, a look of fright present in his eyes. "I . . . thought we'd need somewhere to stay."

"Have you got any money?" she said. "Any gold, any silver?"

Rut continued to stare into her eyes, and then, without warning, a smile sprung up on his lips. "I was hoping you might be able to help with that."

19

NOR'TARTH

HILDIE SOON LEARNED, as Rut relayed his discussion with the man to her, that the town where they found themselves was known as Nor'tarth.

Rut spoke at length, constantly slipping her sidelong glances, as if searching for approval; to know that he'd done the right thing.

Well, if Hildie was totally honest, she wasn't all that pleased with his handling of the man who'd offered them lodgings for the night. She certainly didn't have anything to pay with and—from what Rut had said—it was clear that he didn't.

That left just the little girl, and Hildie doubted *she* had anything.

It was only while they'd walked their way through the side streets, on their way to the tavern, that Hildie had had the presence of mind to take stock of the town properly.

And she noticed some very strange things.

For a start, the roofs of the houses were all in the form of ramparts; stone blocks which seemed perfect for archers to position themselves and fire arrows down into the streets below . . . actually, it reminded Hildie somewhat of the streets of Ilsnare. The ones which led up to the Palace. How those labyrinthine side streets were intended to leave any prospective invaders feeling deeply disorientated—confused that they seemed unable to arrive at the Palace Gates.

And all the while archers and crossbowmen would fire on them from above; from what—the invaders' scouts and spies had reported to be—innocuous-looking uptown houses.

Hildie wondered if the same architect had visited Nor'tarth.

Next, Hildie noticed how the windows on all of the houses, invariably, had the same thick wooden shutters. These wooden shutters, she saw right away, had slits down the middle. Again, she supposed this design was intended with archers and crossbowmen in mind. One thing was for certain, she wouldn't have liked to lead a siege on this town.

Even with *her* magic it would've proven a great struggle.

"Just up here," Rut said, over his shoulder as he led them through the crowds. "He told me that it's just across the town square."

Hildie brought the little girl closer to her side; seeing the street children hanging around them. She noticed that a few were pointing at the little girl, no doubt putting into motion all sorts of *children's* gossip.

The people in Nor'tarth were, like the Almber, and all those who occupied the tropics; brown skinned. But their facial details were somewhat altered.

The Almber all shared the similar, squashed-nose profile; the rotund face; coupled with the bushy, black eyebrows and thatch of matching hair.

But the residents of Nor'tarth appeared to have more in common with the citizens of Ilsnare: thinner features, squarer jaws, fairer hair, and—Hildie noticed—many towering figures among them. Although the Almber had been many things, one thing they certainly hadn't been was tall.

As they crossed the town square, Hildie took in the smooth, white marble building which stood over everything else. She remarked at the pillars which propped it up; and then the steps which led up to the entrance.

She couldn't quite remember having seen something so beautiful created by Mortals.

If it—*indeed*—had been created by Mortals.

All the townspeople gathered about in groups, congregating in the town square.

Already Hildie noted the great difference between Nor'tarth and Ilsnare, where the Royal Guards made a point of clearing the streets after nightfall.

Being found out in the darkness in Ilsnare was a recipe for being hassled by the authorities; and if the authorities didn't get you then the common thieves would.

Clearly the people of Nor'tarth didn't share these concerns.

And it felt almost as if a weight was lifting itself up off Hildie's shoulders to note this.

Strangely, she felt almost as if she was at home here.

As if she had no reason to be frightened.

Everybody seemed so *happy* and *contented*.

She wondered if it might be something in the water . . .

Rut led them over the town square and to the other side of the plaza.

He glanced about and then squinted up at one of the signs—written out in the local dialect so as to be almost incomprehensible to Hildie.

He looked back at her and the little girl, smiled and then led them in through the doorway to what was—in theory—to be their lodgings for the night.

It was then that Hildie felt the little girl's fingers slip away from her own.

Soon enough, she found herself grasping only thin air.

She pivoted on the spot—gaped at the area surrounding her.

But there was no sign of the little girl.

At the back of her mind, almost, Hildie heard the *chink* of something falling on the cobblestones at her feet. When she turned her attention downward, she saw an object sparkle in the torchlight.

Her heart hung in her throat.

It rapped hard for several seconds.

Then she ducked down to retrieve the glittering object.

Only when she held it in her right hand, when she turned it over and watched how the golden dust embedded in the glass glittered in the torchlight did she realise what it was.

How it had been produced.

In Almber's Bay . . . she had created this strange sort of glass . . . when she'd cast that firestorm which'd consumed everything in sight.

Caused so much destruction.

And yet it had created this *beautiful* thing.

Holding the glass to her chest, she turned on the spot.

Gazed about.

But she couldn't see the little girl.

20

HEFFERS TAVERN

W HEN HILDIE STEPPED IN over the threshold, she could hear nothing but hurried conversations. Her cheeks were flushed from her constant searches through the crowds.

She and Rut had spent the best part of the last hour looking for the little girl, but they hadn't been able to locate her.

In the end, they'd seen no other option except to return here.

To Heffers Tavern . . . where Rut had—*apparently*—booked them a room for the night.

Hildie continued to cling to the piece of glass embedded with golden dust which'd turned up when the girl had disappeared. She couldn't help wondering if the girl had been carrying the glass with her during the entirety of the journey from Almber's Bay. Although Hildie had been close to the girl, she couldn't recall having caught sight of the glass at any time . . . and the little girl had been holding her hand the whole while *too* . . . the way that the girl had skipped along in her own apparently absent-minded way didn't seem to square with her keeping this piece of glass hidden beneath her top.

But what other explanation was there?

The whole tavern was abuzz with conversation, and the odour of honey ale. Hildie felt her gut tremor a little as she caught the taste of pork at the back of her throat.

She was hungry . . . *starving* actually.

As they approached the front desk—an elegant, well-polished affair with a stack of parchment piled up on its surface, and a pristine female attendant behind it—Hildie couldn't help wondering if Rut had managed to pick out just about the most exclusive, most *expensive*, set of lodgings in the entire town.

With this thought on her mind, and the ridiculous prospect of them checking in without having so much as a pair of pennies to rub together, she tugged on Rut's sleeve.

But it was too late.

Rut was already speaking with the attendant at the desk.

Why did he have to just go along with everything so easily? He was like one of those dim-witted fish which the Almber would often catch, dozing away in the sun-baked shallows.

Hildie stood to one side while the female attendant took note of their names on a roll of parchment. It was only when the woman finally tilted her head back and cast a glance across the two of them that a look of doubt appeared across her face.

She had properly absorbed their clothing.

And their current condition.

Hildie was surprised that the attendant hadn't *smelled* them the second they'd crossed the threshold.

This was, apparently, Rut's cue to lean in over the desk, lower the tone of his voice and mumble something about King Louson.

For a long second, Hildie was certain that the woman was going to take the comment as if it was nothing at all . . . as if she believed this bedraggled-looking pair—who'd obviously been out on the plains for the past few nights and were *clearly* deranged— actually did have some sort of a connection to the King of Shel- lacnass.

Then the woman flashed a glance over their heads.

When Hildie followed the woman's gaze, she saw that a pair of guards had appeared there; ones who, if they'd been there before, Hildie hadn't noticed at all.

They were large, with shoulder-length hair.

Both of them wore leather armour and a scimitar at the waist.

Hildie supposed this was the way that Nor'tarth kept its inhab- itants so happy—so *contented*.

It was only as the guards were closing on them that the female attendant spoke up.

"Excuse me," she said, with that same, strange backwater accent the man who Rut had spoken to had possessed.

Hildie turned back to the female attendant. She was expecting the attendant to be wearing a wry smile and to have a witty put- down on the tip of her tongue; something along the lines of, 'Thank you, but we don't need *your* kind here'.

Instead, though, the attendant's gaze remained fixed on Hildie's chest.

Hildie felt an itchy sensation pass over the surface of her skin. She hated it when people looked at her. She supposed that she had got out of the habit of civilisation—of *society*—and that she had relished being the one to play the observer.

But, right now, she was centre stage.

"What's that?" the female attendant said. "What've you got there?"

A shudder passed through Hildie's gut, and then she recalled that she was clinging to the piece of glass with the golden dust embedded in it.

As if Hildie had just noticed the glass herself, she held it up before her gaze; taking care, as always, to keep her mutilated left hand down at her side and out of sight.

"Uh, I . . ." Hildie began, but didn't finish.

Before Hildie could act, the female attendant got up from behind the desk, skittered across the floor of the tavern and disappeared through a doorway.

Where she'd gone, Hildie had no way of guessing.

When she looked back to the doorway, to the guards there, she saw that they continued to hold them in a stern gaze.

Hildie couldn't shift the idea that they might be about to get themselves into some deep trouble. And, from Hildie's experiences with deep trouble, she knew that it often led to her being put in a gaol for the night.

Hildie wasn't convinced that she'd fully recovered her magical strength following the outpouring at Almber's Bay.

The one which had—*apparently*—created this piece of glass with golden dust embedded she now held in her good right hand.

Before Hildie had a chance to turn to Rut, to suggest that they, perhaps, skitter on out into the streets and, surreptitiously, skip town, the attendant reappeared in the doorway.

This time, she had an elderly man in tow.

Hildie took him in.

His long, white hair; his fluffy beard—*fluffier* eyebrows—and how he wore a flowing, royal-purple robe. He walked with his hands clenched behind his back and Hildie noted that he had silver-blue eyes . . . or were they, in fact, as white as his hair?

The female attendant looked to Hildie and Rut once more, and it was only now that Hildie thought to look at her properly; to see that on the end of a golden chain, dangling down over the front of the algae-green blouse the attendant wore, and which matched her eyes, there was a small piece of glass. Golden dust embedded within.

As if Hildie had just uttered some secret password, a smile tweaked the attendant's lips. She nodded as if replying to a question which Hildie hadn't even asked.

"We've waited such a long time," she said. "*Such* a long time to see this again."

Deciding that she should play the fool here—and, to tell the truth, she wasn't that far off *being* the fool in any case—Hildie responded, "To see what?"

The attendant nodded to Hildie's right hand, where she held the piece of glass. "To see *that*," the attendant replied.

Hildie now turned her attention back to the elderly man who the attendant had brought out of the woodwork. She could tell from the way his cheeks flourished with burst capillaries that he had been drinking . . . or that he had done a great deal of drinking in the past.

The elderly man didn't say a word. He only reached for the half-moon spectacles which dangled down around his neck. He perched them on the tip of his nose.

His silver eyes grew round as the lenses magnified them.

He squinted hard and worry lines appeared in his brow.

Finally, apparently done with his inspection, he slipped his glasses off his nose, allowing them to fall back down to their previous position on his chest, where they hung off their silver-bead chain.

"They're gone," he said.

Without warning, he turned his eyes onto Hildie's, then added, "*Aren't* they?"

21

AWAY FROM THE MADNESS

R UT STOOD UP in one of the back corridors of Heffers
Tavern.

He stared at the wooden panelling on the walls and then to the
framed charcoal pieces of art. They were the sorts of etchings that
he would often see the Hobblesmen bring through his village
when he was a boy.

Bleak. Pit-black tones. *Bleaker* subject matter.

When he analysed them he saw that they depicted a whole
array of destitute moments.

A hanging.

A wolf being gored by a Mortal hunting party.

Thunderclouds moving in over a distant city.

Ilsnare?

The Crystal City?

Rut turned away from the charcoal drawings, and shifted a

glance across the corridor to the firmly shut walnut door; the door behind which Hildie and the elderly man had disappeared.

More than anything, Rut wanted to go out into the streets and search for the little girl; the girl who had come to him in the sand gaol . . . and who had come to him afterwards; when Hildie had been working her magic. He thought back to what the little girl had said.

That he wasn't to trust Hildie.

Well, that was a no-brainer.

How did that little girl *believe* that he could ever trust the person responsible for burning down his village; for destroying the little family he had left?

He would never forget.

And he would never *trust* her.

Rut wondered why Lou had entrusted him to go and fetch Hildie; if she really needed to be fetched at all. It was obvious that trouble was coming—that it was headed for Ilsnare. Why else would Lou send for Hildie; why else would he want to bring back such an unstable—*yet potent*—weapon?

But couldn't Lou have sent Sully after Hildie, here—to the tropics?

Then again, despite everything, despite having to *be around* Hildie, Rut supposed that he much preferred being here, in the tropics, to heading north and into the Winter's Moan; where Sully had been sent, for who-knew-what reason.

Rut felt a rumble at the base of his stomach.

He was starving, and his legs ached so much that they hurt.

He knew he needed rest.

Although the little girl continued to play on his mind, he knew —*somehow*—that she would be okay. That, just as she had slipped away into nothingness before, she would be able to pull the very same trick again.

Wherever she had disappeared, he was certain that she would be back.

He *hoped* she would be back.

Just to think about their journey here, to Nor'tarth, and how Hildie had fawned over the little girl; how she'd hardly allowed her out of her sight, almost constantly clinging to the little girl's hand with her good right hand.

The little girl had seemed to bring out a softness in Hildie.

Had seemed to make her almost less *scary* . . .

But Rut pushed that feeling away.

He had allowed himself to be so afraid in the past. He had permitted his Mortal fears to have control of him. But he wouldn't allow them any longer.

With the dangers up ahead—with the danger that seemed to lurk about every corner of the kingdom—he would need to be brave.

If he ever wished to return home.

To his wife and daughter.

To Emelda and Forre.

As Rut smelled the roast pork wafting about the corridor, all through the air which surrounded him, he tuned himself out of the *babble* which carried up the stairs with the delicious scent.

At the end of the corridor, there was a large window; one of those windows which opened very much like a door . . . out onto a balcony.

For some reason, Rut found himself drawn to the glass.

He trod toward it.

Pressed his forehead up against the surface; feeling the gentle chill against his skin.

He peered across the rooftops, with their curious, turreted design; and then out beyond the glowing, orange lights of the streets to the plains beyond.

He believed he could almost make out the silvery glow of moonlight on the sea which sat on the horizon. But he couldn't be sure.

The glass seemed almost to block his view, so he reached for the brass handle and pressed it firmly downward. The hinge gave a slight *squeak* as he pushed the door away from him, and out onto the balcony.

Rut stood up on the stone balcony—like the rest of the town with a rampart-like design. The *babble* of conversation from within the tavern became dampened, and he could only make out the *clickety-clack* of carts moving over the cobblestone streets; the gentle *snorting* of the odd horse here and there.

As he clung onto the edge of the stone rampart, he peered out through the gap.

He could better make out the horizon now.

The silvery moonlight playing with the waves of the sea.

It *was* the sea, wasn't it?

What else could it be?

22

AWE-STRUCK

THE ROOM WAS BOXY, and the bookshelves were filled to bursting with sun-faded, leather-bound tomes; the types with gilded edges to the pages. A window, no larger than the visor on an iron helmet, provided the only ventilation.

The only respite from the clamouring dust which seemed to creep out from every nook and cranny and invade Hildie's airways like some sort of malicious phantom.

Hildie stared across the table at the elderly man; at the man who had introduced himself—simply—as Keamard.

She hadn't told him her name; the same routine she practised almost unconsciously with strangers . . . with anybody who she had just met.

And she had no intention of giving her name—her *real* name —until it became absolutely necessary.

From somewhere, the elderly man had produced a lamp, which sent an uneven, flickering glow about the near-windowless room. Although Hildie had done her best to hang onto the piece of glass for as long as she possibly could, she had eventually —*reluctantly*—relented and allowed the man to prise it from the fingers of her good right hand.

As the man stooped low over the object, a magnifying glass clenched in his fist, Hildie could almost feel the impatience seeping out of every pore.

Didn't he know that she and Rut had been travelling all day?

That the only thing they wanted to do was lay their heads down?

. . . Perhaps after having indulged themselves in some of that succulent-smelling pork downstairs; and, no doubt, at least in Rut's case, the honey ale which seemed to be sourced from some never-ending, subterranean stream.

Hildie had vaguely hoped that in all her time away from society she might lose the somewhat polite manners she'd always been afflicted with . . . but, unfortunately, it seemed as if she was stricken worse than ever.

So, as 'Keamard' inspected the artefact which she had had a hand in creating, Hildie clung to the shadows which surrounded the table, quietly sulking and wishing that he would get over with his inspection as soon as possible.

Just as with all men of a certain age when they stumbled across something 'remarkable' from the natural world, Keamard emitted an awfully large amount of *umms* and *ahhs!* as if some sort of comprehension had up and bit him.

Perhaps what Hildie resented most about these routines was that they seemed specifically designed so as to make her feel ignorant.

But, for all Hildie cared, these men could all go off into the undergrowth, go about pinning butterflies or scooping up hand-fuls of pebbles all they liked. They could even call it Knowledge if they really wanted to. Still, she didn't see why she had to pay them any mind.

Finally, after it seemed like hours had passed by, Keamard straightened up, his spine creaking as he did so. With a slight smile which sprouted a whole series of wrinkles about his eyes, he shook his head and said, "Yes, this is *exactly* it . . . exactly what I thought it was."

"And what's *that*?" Hildie said, unable to keep the bile out of her tone.

Keamard set his magnifying glass down on the table top, glanced briefly to the piece of glass, and then he reached up and massaged the bridge of his nose. "Almber's Glass," he replied.

Somehow, Hildie didn't feel a great amount of surprise.

It followed.

She decided to ask the pertinent question. "Rare, is it?"

Keamard's smile widened and a flicker of light crossed his silver eyes. He gave a slight chuckle; one of those which, without fail, when it came from an elderly man, made her feel about as foolish as a girl only seven summers old.

"Oh, certainly," Keamard replied. "The Almber are an *extremely* jealous people; at least when considering the manner in which they keep their gold guarded."

Hildie turned her mind back to the Almber, and how they would treat intruders.

She couldn't help but feel, after spending so much time with them, that 'jealousy' was the wrong sentiment. But she didn't think to correct Keamard, not wanting to give away too much all at once.

Keamard continued, "Often we hear about the attempts of Mortals to breach Almber's Bay—not far from here—and to come away with just a sprinkling of the golden dust which adorns their beaches." He shook his head then chuckled again. "But Mortals do not usually possess the required abilities to come away from Almber's Bay with what they seek." The smile which'd lingered on his lips throughout the entire exchange waivered slightly. "One of the very hardest of all things is to capture the honey from the bees' own hive."

"But it can be done," Hildie said. "The girl—downstairs—her necklace?"

Keamard pouted. "Yes, my daughter . . . she had an, uh, *admirer* once, and he brought her that." He gave a flourish of his hand. "When my daughter passed away she handed it onto her own daughter; my granddaughter. The girl downstairs."

Hildie noted how Keamard's expression turned a little sour at this memory. She decided to change the subject. "So who *would* be capable of stealing the honey from the hive?"

Keamard's expression cleared. He peered at Hildie closely then said, "Ah, well, that would be the question, would it not?"

"Magical beings . . . *Creatures*?" Hildie said, still not wanting to say anything which might incriminate her . . . something which she might not be able to explain away later.

"Yes," Keamard said, turning his attention back downward, to the glass on the table before him. "They would be far more subtle in their approach; they would perhaps have the strength to overwhelm the Almber . . . to use their magic against them."

Here, almost out of nowhere, Keamard snapped his neck upward to stare hard into Hildie's eyes. His lips parted as if he was about to bark out the accusation which, Hildie was sure, had been etched on the forefront of his mind throughout their meeting.

But, before he got the chance to utter so much as a sound, there was a pounding at the door.

Hildie and Keamard turned to look.

And then the bells started ringing.

23

SIEGE

HILDIE'S HEART bounced about her chest.

It tickled her throat.

Blood pumped to her temples.

Sweat leaked from her brow.

She found herself swept up by the madness; the people pouring out of every room of the tavern; some of them half dressed . . . women wrapped only in bedsheets; their men stumbling to hoik their boots up over their bare feet.

As she clambered her way down the now-busy staircase, she concentrated on putting one foot in front of the other, having lost the presence of mind to hide her afflicted left hand.

Because of all the people rushing past, she had to spend all her energy on concentrating on gripping the banister tightly with her sole hand. As she helped herself down the staircase, she remembered that she'd left the Almber's Glass behind . . . that she had forgotten it on the table.

She tried to turn around, but people bundled into her constantly, in an obvious hurry to get downstairs. It was almost as if she was attempting to swim upstream.

She could feel Rut just behind her, and although he was surely as panicked as the rest of the inhabitants of the tavern, she was glad that he'd found the required bravery to stay with her.

To keep her company.

The elderly man, Keamard, though, had shot off to some other part of the tavern; jabbering something about being 'unprepared'.

When Hildie reached the bottom floor of the tavern, she toyed with the idea of the open doorway; leading out onto the street outside. Nobody resident in the tavern was headed for the exit, and after a couple of moments of standing still to stare, she saw *why*.

Bells tolled, announcing the crisis.

Men, women and children seemed to shout from one side of the city to the other in their local dialect. Although Hildie had trouble distinguishing and making sense of the individual words, she could easily understand the panic which was taut in the air.

The night-time streets thronged with people running this way and that; some of them lugging along spears, or crossbows—bows and arrows.

A few already had on rudimentary leather armour . . . still fewer wore iron chest plates and brandished broadswords.

From what Hildie could see of the streets, there was just as much panic outside as there was within Heffers Tavern.

And, as the people seemed to be rushing along an established route, deeper into the tavern, Hildie decided that this would be her best hope of salvation . . . from whatever it was that was going on.

Finally, following the flow of the people, she came across an open doorway which led downward, into the innards of the tavern. She glanced back, saw that Rut was still on her heels, and the two of them entered behind the other people.

The stairs leading down into the tavern basement were not as well-constructed as those which led to the upper floors; which was to say that, instead of being made of stone, they were nothing much more than dug out of the muddy underground.

Already, whenever Hildie breathed in, she could smell the dank scent of soil; and she could feel its dampness pressing up against her skin.

Something about that odour, about the *feel* of soil around her, sent a shudder skittering through her blood. She supposed that it had something to do with being afraid of death . . . it seemed unavoidable to think that her corpse might be committed to the cold, unfeeling ground forevermore.

At the back of her mind, Hildie had always hoped that she might die in flames.

In the same way her father had done.

Magic tearing her apart from the inside out.

When they reached the bottom of the basement, and Hildie heard the slight *squelch* of mud beneath the tread of her boots, she felt Rut's reassuring hand guiding her from the lower back. He eased her away from the massed-up people and into a corner.

Somebody, somewhere, lit up a torch. Refreshing—*tingling*—flames flickered about the gloom of the basement sending the fire magic within Hildie's veins surging toward her heart. It sent fresh energy cutting through her.

And made her feel powerful.

Finally, she turned on Rut. "What's going on?" she said, the glass still clutched to her chest.

Rut's eyes skittered about the crowd as if attempting to divine some sort of incoming threat—as if he could see through walls. Then he turned back to Hildie, met her eye for a second, and dropped his voice to a near whisper. "Outside," he said, "while I was up on the balcony, I saw them."

"Saw *who*?" Hildie replied.

Rut's voice got quieter and huskier still. "Those Creatures . . . from Almber's Bay . . . the *Horrox*."

Hildie felt her whole body go rigid.

She thought back to the village they had passed through on their way here—the village where they had got the water for the remainder of their journey to Nor'tarth.

The dead bodies.

All those *ravished* bodies.

When she turned back to Rut, it seemed as if they had the same thought on their minds, but Hildie was the only one who could find the words. "You don't think . . ." she managed to get out before, from within the crowd, someone raised their voice.

At first, Hildie believed it was a man speaking; the first tones of the voice were so guttural, so indentured with power. But, when she finally got a proper look at the figure standing at the top of the basement steps, she realised it was the female attendant from the tavern front desk.

She still had on the algae-green blouse, and the piece of Almber's Glass which she wore dangling from her neck reflected the steady torchlight. "They're back again," she said, this time with her voice fraying a little; the gravelly tone lost to a couple of breaking points . . . but she managed to keep up the same power.

"Down here you'll all be safe; and—with the gods' will—we shall defeat them just as we have done before."

There was some mumbling among the crowd but nobody spoke up.

What was there to say?

Finally, the female attendant—Keamard's granddaughter—disappeared back up the staircase, headed for the tavern itself.

Maybe she was going to take up a crossbow or bow and arrows and repel the invaders.

When Hildie turned back to Rut, he said, "I don't understand, why don't they build city walls?"

Hildie felt the dawning realisation pass over her.

She thought back to all the rampart-like designs of the rooftops.

To how the wooden shutters all had slits for firing arrows through.

"The whole city," she replied. "The whole city is a fortress."

24

HIDING OUT

SOON ENOUGH, the tavern basement became too hot to stand.

While before it had felt as if the walls were leaking chilly morning dew, now it was as if they perspired like a hog.

Hildie breathed in the stink of the people; some of them sozzled in ale, and others in the odours of intimacy. Pungent perfume cut through everything. It burned Hildie's nostril hair, and sent her heart leaping up to the back of her throat.

Several times, tavern hands came down from above carrying buckets of water and mugs to be passed around. Hildie heard the cries of several males among them for more ale to be brought to the basement, but *those* requests went unanswered.

And she was glad for it.

Few things were worse than being forced into sharing a confined area with many people, but one of those things was if said people were drunk out of their skulls.

Hildie and Rut settled down in the corner of the basement; the two of them leaning their backs up against the exposed wall of soil.

Hildie wondered what she must look like now.

Ever since she'd left Almber's Bay behind, she'd not had a single chance to change into something more decent than the floaty, white dress she wore. Although she hadn't had a chance to look at herself in a mirror, she could only imagine how her white dress had been reduced to soot and sweat. Whenever she looked down over herself, she could tell that there were several tears in dire need of a seamstress.

If she hadn't been in the tropics, she supposed she might've frozen to death during the nights.

Just those cold thoughts sent a skitter through her veins.

Her fire magic kept her body constantly warm.

It refused to let her die.

What struck Hildie most about being down in the basement of the tavern was the lack of information from above. Although she hardly expected to hear stilted battle cries—the *twang* of bow strings rebounding as arrows flew—she *had* thought that she would at least hear the damp *clang* of swords meeting or the *clop* of horses' hooves passing over the cobblestones outside.

But there was nothing.

In the end, it was Hildie who broke the silence. "Do you think she's okay?"

Rut—whose eyelids were drooping—suddenly snapped back into alertness.

He looked back at her, and, for a second, Hildie thought she might need to clarify just who she meant. But then he gave her a slight smile and said, "Yes, I think she's fine."

Hildie nodded in response, although she wasn't convinced herself.

In fact, she was on the cusp of rising up off the spot where she sat in the basement and heading up those stairs. Just let them stop her.

Even if she wouldn't be able to track down the little girl, she couldn't shake the thought that she might be able to do something to help with the siege.

That there might be *something* she could do.

Wasn't she a fire mage after all?

Already she felt hatred for these monsters—these *Horrox*—brewing within her; a hatred which she would struggle to control as much as she struggled to control her magic.

They had been responsible for the death of the Almber.

For leaving only one of them alive.

And she was determined that she would make them pay.

It was then that her thoughts turned back on a point Rut had mentioned earlier. She turned to him. "You said they were shape shifters."

Rut mumbled something approaching an acknowledgement.

"Then why're they attacking like this?" she said. "Why wouldn't they find a more subtle way of invading Nor'tarth?"

Rut swallowed hard.

He widened his eyes, and then looked at Hildie closely. "The chances are that they're tired of hiding—that they don't see any reason for living like second-class citizens any longer." He swallowed hard, and his Adam's apple bobbed in his throat. "You see, there've been murmurings . . ."

" 'Murmurings'? " Hildie replied, raising her eyebrows.

"Since you've been gone, there's been a rising wave of support for Creatures—for *all* Magical beings—to be accepted within the Kingdom of Shellacnass, for them to be afforded the same rights and protections offered to Mortals."

"And?" Hildie put in.

Rut gave a slight nod. "Many of them have come together—many of them have begun to form a movement, so that they might demand what they see as their right."

"And they think they'll achieve it with violence?"

Rut shrugged. "Who's to say?" he replied. "I'm Royal Guardian of the Waterways, not Captain of the Royal Guards."

Hildie pressed her back up against the wall of the basement. When she replied, she was deeply aware of her surroundings, that, on all sides—Rut included—she was surrounded by Mortals. She couldn't speak frankly here. She spoke almost to herself, too quietly for Rut to hear. "I don't see why that's such a terrible thing to ask for . . ."

Even if Rut had overheard what she'd said, he wasn't given a chance to respond, because, from the staircase above, she saw that Keamard's granddaughter had appeared once more. She was flushed and she held a bow down at her thigh. When she spoke this time, there was real panic in her voice; it was clear that she was beginning to lose her cool.

"Archers!" she said. "Who here can hold a bow?"

The assembled people in the basement were silent.

Nobody replied.

Keamard's granddaughter flared her eyes at the room. "Who's *sober* here?!"

Hildie was surprised when, without so much as a hint, Rut rose to his feet and held up his hand.

"*I am* . . . and I can hold a crossbow fine—it's the *firing* part that's always been the trouble."

25

A SKULLER PITCHES IN

RUT COULD FEEL his heart thumping against his ribcage. He had no time to think as he pursued the female attendant—the one who had met them at the tavern front desk. She bounded up the staircase ahead of him.

He eyed the bow she held down at her thigh and couldn't help thinking, already, that he had made an enormous mistake in putting himself forward.

He hadn't shot a bow for the best part of a decade. Being Royal Guardian of the Waterways, he had had his own personal escort; four—sometimes *five*—extremely capable men who would do any shooting or slicing that was required.

As it turned out, there really hadn't been all that much need.

Despite the odd, fierce neighbourly struggle, the Royal Guardian of the Waterways rarely got involved in full-blown melees.

Or, in Rut's case, not at all.

They rose to one of the upper floors of the tavern; a floor or two above where they had gone to meet with the elderly man, and from where Rut had observed the incoming invaders. He had barely brought his knuckles down against the door before he heard the clanging of bells begin outside; in the city streets . . . accompanied by the sounds of panic; some shouting, the odd *patter* of shoes over cobblestones; the stirrings of horses woken early from their night-time rest.

The whole scene reminded him of his time as a skuller, when he would wake the whole city because of a breach in the fortifications; something which had allowed in one of the cursed animals. He recalled, himself, being younger than he was now, tucked up in bed and hearing the *clang-clang-clang* of the town bell announcing that everybody should remain indoors if they cared for their lives.

"Here," the female attendant said, indicating a doorway.

Rut glanced to her, and then to the room itself.

It was a small room—a *tight* room—similar to the one Hildie and the elderly man had used to speak about that strange piece of glass. There was a single window which had the shutter drawn.

Only the crack down the centre allowing for anything to pass through it, or—more importantly—*out* of it.

Before Rut had a chance to get his bearings, the female attendant produced a crossbow from somewhere and, along with a leather holster filled with bolts, she shoved it into his chest. "There you go," she said, already leaving him. "Take down as many as you can, okay?"

Rut felt himself blinking back the confusion for several moments, still desperately trying to get a handle on the progress of events up to now. Then—*suddenly, inexplicably*—he snapped back to the present moment.

He clenched the crossbow and bolts tight to his chest and then glanced to the window.

He needed to get on with this.

And he needed to get on with this *now*.

Do everything he could to pitch in.

The decision made, Rut loaded a bolt into his crossbow and then hopped over to the window. He almost tripped over the corner of a rug lying on the floor but, somehow—perhaps because nobody was watching—managed to arrest his natural clumsiness and stay on his feet.

When he reached the niche in the window, he got down on his knees and then peered out, down into the street below.

It was night, of course, and the only light which filled the streets was that of the torches which hung down off the walls. He could see no sign of the Horrox yet. He wondered if they would venture into the town on horseback, or if they would try out a more subtle means.

Owing to the design of the city, it would be possible for them to sneak in from any entrance point and skulk about the streets until they reached their goal.

But where *was* their goal?

What was the building they hoped to conquer?

It was then that Rut felt his mind catch up with him, and he had the good sense to glance up, to the central square on which Heffers Tavern sat.

The streets were eerily empty.

Devoid of either townspeople or the Horrox.

All the same, Rut stared down the bolt he had set into his crossbow; just waiting for one of them to cross his path. This wouldn't be like last time—he wouldn't be running away from the battle—he would be *part* of it.

His finger lingered over the trigger and he slowed down his thought processes, attempting to steady his shaking hands. One thing was for certain, however afraid he might've been as a younger man, his hands had never shaken this much before.

He supposed that was another fact of ageing.

He crouched down at the niche in the wooden shutter, every muscle in his body tight and ready to channel its power into the trigger. He could hardly believe how alone he felt. How he was *alone* in this room at the top of the tavern . . . and yet, he was fighting alongside many hundred—*many thousand?*—invisible allies; all throughout the city.

As he felt many thoughts reel through his mind; not least those which concerned the unknowable worry of whether or not he would *ever* be able to get home again, he spotted the first Horrox turning the corner.

Its skin was red-raw; even in the torchlight he could see that.

Its body stiff and well-muscled.

And its eyes pit black.

Rut sank down onto his haunches, lined up the shot.

And then fired.

26

A MAGE IS A FRIEND INDEED

AS HILDIE LEFT THE BASEMENT BEHIND, she felt as though all those eyes were still fixed upon her. It had been too much. She had only been able to stand being alone down there, in the basement, for less than five minutes after Rut had taken off and left.

Although she told herself that the reason she'd voluntarily left the safety of the basement behind was because she didn't want Rut to have to fight alone—without an ally as useful as *she*—the real reason was that she wanted to locate that little girl.

She wondered if the little girl had gone off with those street children they'd seen when they'd arrived to the town. And that only set Hildie's worries firing all the more.

Because those children might not have homes.

They might not *have* anywhere to go.

Nowhere to hide.

The tavern was strangely quiet, and she assumed that Rut had headed upstairs, to one of the upper rooms where he was tending to a crossbow. There was nobody to halt her progress toward the door of the tavern, and she made short work of lifting the wooden barricade which some well-meaning employee of the establishment had placed across the door.

Didn't they realise who they were dealing with here?

That these were *Magical* beings?

That, if they so wished, they could blow out every last door in town?

. . . Or was it simply a dead-duck gesture; a sort of measure that someone might take when, knowing that they can do nothing, they might as well do *something*.

Then again, she supposed that wherever it was the Horrox were headed, that it didn't involve indiscriminately blowing doors off their hinges.

Hildie held herself still, feeling the tingle of fire magic through her entire body; all that energy just raring to go. She was about to walk in weakness, too. To walk out in the moonlight . . . and she was taking a risk in assuming that her powers would have recovered from their previous use; when she had slaughtered both that band of Horrox and the Almber.

Would her magic be crying out for more?

Would it be crying out for more *blood*?

. . . Perhaps if it was then she could fool herself into believing that this was the 'good' thing she had always waited for—that if she could just harness her powers and *channel* them that she could save all these innocent people from danger.

From these Magical beings.

Once Hildie was out on the street, she felt a cool night-time breeze blowing.

It brushed up against her cheeks and ruffled her red hair a little.

She tugged the strands back behind her ears.

Then she turned her attention to the Horrox.

She saw them entering the town square, on the other side; from out of side streets.

They didn't ride horses tonight, and they appeared unarmed.

But that didn't stop the archers and crossbow men from raining their arrows and bolts down on them. The sound of the projectiles was smooth and sharp; and they were invisible against the night-time sky.

Horrox slumped down and died on the streets, almost casually, with a degree of stoicism that her father—Ma'reygar—might've demanded from his magical army. It was incredible to think of the pain the Horrox must be suffering from those stray arrows and bolts; catching them in their flanks, or in their arms.

In some cases in their heads.

But they kept on coming.

A steady march.

Headed for one place.

Headed toward Hildie.

It was the town hall which Hildie had held in her sights before realising that fact, and she still struggled to believe what her brain informed her.

That the Horrox really were headed toward where she stood.

Their beady, black eyes fixed on her.

Dozens of them . . . perhaps hundreds more to come . . . they had all run the gauntlet through so many other armoured streets —just like this one—so that they might reach this point.

So that they might get *this* close to her.

And now they were this close, what did they want?

To destroy her, surely?

Perhaps they knew—perhaps they knew *all about* what'd happened at Almber's Bay, and that she was the one responsible. It wasn't like it would be difficult to know that the resulting massacre of both the Horrox and the Almber had been the result of an enraged fire mage.

The world had seen the likes of Ma'reygar before; enough so that it might be able to instantly recognise the work of his daughter.

Still, even as the Horrox advanced on her, even as she felt her fingertips tingling with fire magic as it rose to the surface, Hildie found herself thinking about the little girl.

Wondering where she was now.

And if she was safe.

27

FIRE!

R UT CONTINUED to pump away on his crossbow, shoving in bolt after bolt; watching his projectiles join the never-ending, inky-black stream raining down on the Horrox.

But it was no good.

There were just too many of them.

And they kept on coming.

He watched on, feeling a rising sickness in his gut as the red-skinned Horrox trod all over their fallen comrades in their constant advance.

And Rut couldn't help thinking that they were headed here.

That they were headed *right for* the tavern.

But why?

He pulled his crossbow free of the niche in the wooden window shutter for a moment and then flashed a glance back across the square.

The town hall was on the other side of the street.

Surely, if they believed that they had a chance of taking the town they would make that their number-one target?

Rut shifted himself around, brought himself side-on so that he might get a better view through the narrow slit in the wooden shutter. He stared into the street directly below, to the cobblestones which now ran with the black blood of the Horrox.

The Horrox were crowding around . . . *something* . . . forming a semi-circle, almost as a group of hunters might corner a wounded deer.

He knew, without mistake, that they were moving in on the kill.

That, if he didn't do something, they *would* kill.

Rut shoved his crossbow back through the slit in the shutter and fired off several more bolts. When he pulled back from the slit, he saw that another few of the Horrox lay dead in the streets, although he couldn't confirm that they had indeed been 'his' kills . . . there were so many arrows and bolts arcing through the air that it was impossible to tell one from the other.

As Rut stood back from the shutter once again, it was as if the Horrox read his mind and relented. They gave him a look at the person they had cornered.

Up against the wall of the tavern.

For several seconds, Rut simply couldn't believe it.

But his heart responded.

It stopped beating.

And then kicked harder than ever.

Hildie!

Rut brought his crossbow up to the slit in the wooden shutter with a renewed vigour.

Despite everything—despite the fact she'd burned down his

village; killed those he loved—he knew that Lou was counting on him; that he had to bring her back to Ilsnare.

If not . . . well, he didn't want to think about it . . .

It was only when he stopped his rapid-fire shots, when he pulled away from the shutter for what felt as though it would be the final time, that he noticed Hildie was on her feet; and that she was walking among the Horrox.

That they seemed to be almost *protecting* her . . .

Or was she protecting *them*?

A command rattled through the air. An acknowledgement that the Horrox were headed away from the town square? Away from the tavern?

Or was it because they realised a Mortal was among the Horrox?

Whatever it happened to be, the crossbowmen and archers all waited patiently.

And as Rut turned his attention to the crooked alleyway through which the Horrox were retreating—with Hildie among them—he realised that all the other bows and crossbows had halted their attack. That they were *allowing* the Horrox to flee.

That they believed they'd won the battle.

. . . And, well, they had . . .

Hadn't they?

28

ENEMY OR ALLY?

H ILDIE COULD FEEL the warmth from the rising sun.
And the fresh morning air against her cheeks.

There was the wonderful scent of a fruity broth cooking away; freshly baked bread, too.

To say that Hildie was exhausted would have been nothing but the truth. She hadn't slept properly now for what seemed like days and days. And yet, she couldn't help but feel invigorated.

She sat down on the soft grass and peered across the rolling sand dunes—sprinkled with bushy foliage—to the town of Nor'-tarth on the horizon.

It was hard to believe all the distance she had travelled in just these few days.

Even when she'd been travelling alone, she'd never put so many miles under her feet.

Under her long-suffering boots.

She turned her attention to the encampments; all the organised tarps on this hillside. She wondered how the scouts of Nor'-tarth had failed to spot this enemy location . . . or perhaps they preferred to pretend that it didn't exist at all.

Perhaps they believed their town defences infallible.

Who was Hildie to say?

Nearby, she located the source of the delicious breakfast smells; what she believed to be a female Horrox—she hadn't yet learned how to tell the difference—her thin, muscular frame arched as she stooped over a pot bubbling away over a crackling campfire.

She couldn't wait.

It had been a long night and she was half starving.

As she stared off across the plains, she thought about what had occurred the night before; about how she'd gone out into the streets of Nor'tarth with the determination that she would bring the Horrox to justice.

That she would punish them for what they had caused *her* to do to the Almber.

But when she had gone outside the tavern everything had changed.

She could still hear the words, within her mind, the ones which'd been said so clearly and succinctly, as if they had been spoken in a clear voice, right in her ear.

They had told her that they sought only her, and that if she was to go with them they would abandon their plans to lay siege to Nor'tarth.

They would leave the town alone for evermore.

What else could Hildie have said?

She had wanted to stop the fighting between the townspeople and the Horrox, and she had been successful. A peaceful solution had been arranged.

She wondered if this might be the first problem she had managed to solve without violence . . . quite possibly . . .

She had been told to rest, but she found it impossible to switch off her brain now that she breathed in all the smells of the delicious breakfast being cooked up.

Her hunger vastly overwhelmed her desire for sleep.

As Hildie sat on the grassy hillside, she saw that the female Horrox was bringing her over a wooden bowl of what looked like a kind of porridge, with all sorts of fruits and nuts mixed into it. She recalled that she had often joked about those who ate porridge, saying that they were on a 'horse's diet', but she wasn't joking now as her eyes got wider and wider with each step the wooden bowl closed on her.

She could hardly believe it when she held the warm, wooden bowl in her hands and was able to breathe in the intensely thick aroma. The female Horrox supplied her with a spoon too, and once Hildie had everything she needed, she wasted no time in putting the porridge away. And she only felt truly satisfied after she had had four helpings; with the Horrox each time coming to her and, with a gentle smile, depositing yet more in the wooden bowl.

Hildie had to admit that although she had taken the Horrox for little short of monsters the first time she'd set eyes on them, back at Almber's Bay, she couldn't help but notice a slight charm in their lizard-like snouts; and the horns which grew out of their skin. They didn't seem malicious at all . . . at least she had seen far *more* malicious beings . . .

But best of all was the swilling sensation in her blood, how she could feel her fire magic bubbling about her body, leaving her in a slight daze because it was so strong.

So *potent.*

It reminded her how much she'd missed being around other Magical beings.

Almost as if she *fed* off their magic . . . she wondered if they fed off *hers.*

Once she'd finished with her breakfast, the female Horrox took Hildie's bowl away, apparently to go and wash it in a nearby stream.

As Hildie sat there, alone on the hillside, she pulled her feet free of her boots and rolled her bare toes and the soles of her feet through the long, cleansing grass.

Perhaps she wasn't meant to be around Mortals.

That might just be it.

Why was it that she felt more placid now than she had at any other time in her near past?

Just as Hildie felt the calming waves of sleep begin to kneed their way into her mind, she heard a voice; clean and crisp and clear.

In her mind.

— *Hilda. Thank you for joining with us.*

Hildie turned her head.

Standing there was a Horrox, of course, but this one was much, much larger than the average. He put Hildie in mind of the Horrox she had seen the Almber slay, back on the beach. When the Horrox had demonstrated a lack of knowledge of the Almber customs . . . of how any sort of violent gesture might be interpreted to be an act of aggression, and dealt with accordingly.

His long, lizard-like snout protruded from his face in a proud manner and his black eyes blinked as he inspected her with an obvious—and *profound*—intelligence.

Although Hildie hadn't communicated with her mind for a long time . . . at least since before her communication with the Horrox who'd led her off last night . . . she found that it came just as naturally as all the practice she'd put in over the year would've suggested.

— *It's a pleasure. I only wanted to do the right thing.*

The Horrox circled Hildie's spot several times, looked to Hildie for permission, and then, like a dog finding just the right position in its wicker basket, he lowered himself down; on his knees, in an almost penitent way.

The Horrox took several moments to get completely comfortable. He shrugged his shoulders several times, apparently to loosen the muscles, and then he stared long and hard into her eyes.

Speaking, again, into her mind.

— *For a long time we were admirers of your father's abilities. He was a good friend to us, and this is the reason we sought you out. We believed you to be someone we can trust.*

Hildie focussed on those impossibly still, black eyes—almost like twin drops of blood, brought welling up from the surface of the skin with a pinprick.

Then she spoke back to him.

— *My father was friends with many in the Magical community. But we're very different people.*

Here Hildie sensed, from the Horrox's emotions, that he found this somewhat amusing. She drew her mind back from the Horrox's in a way which she hoped he would find distasteful. From what he said next, he seemed to pick up on the hint.

— *Forgive me, Hilda, but I know what happened at Almber's Bay. I have scouts all over this terrain. In fact, I half hoped that you would react in the way you did there. It showed us your true nature.*

Again, Hildie drew herself back from the Horrox's mind, and could feel herself growing angry.

— *It was an accident! I wanted to protect the Almber, that was all; and the only way I could deal with the threat was with . . .*

There was a long pause as Hildie realised that she couldn't keep speaking, that she couldn't keep lying to herself. She was fully responsible for what she had done.

There was no way around it.

In the end, she spoke into the Horrox's mind again; taking pains to make her tone sound final and decided.

— *I never wanted to hurt them; the blood of the Almber is on your hands.*

The Horrox tilted his head slightly to one side, as if considering a point of view he had previously left unexamined, and then he replied:

— *The Almber's legacy is assured.*

— *'The Almber's legacy is assured'?*

This time, instead of speaking into Hildie's mind, the Horrox gave a slight grunt. Then he turned around and looked off over his shoulder, as if suddenly interested in some element of the encampments.

When he turned back to Hildie, he wore a slight smile across his lizard's lips.

And he spoke into her mind once again.

— *We have searched for you for the longest time, Hilda, and now that we have you among us I would like us to make a deal.*

— *A 'deal'?*

— *Yes.*

Hildie found herself looking out over the encampments once again, out to Nor'tarth on the horizon. She had gone with the Horrox last night so that she might save some lives for once. She hadn't done so with the idea that the Horrox might make her hold to whatever promise her father had given them.

She wouldn't suffer for what her father had done.

But, at the same time, where would she go next?

Where would she *travel* to next?

. . . Where could she go where Louson Dorf, and his minions, wouldn't be able to track her down?

She turned back to the Horrox.

— *What do you propose?*

29

BACK IN NOR'TARTH

STRANGELY, Rut found himself at a loose end the day after Hildie had left town with the Horrox.

Due, in part, to his 'brave' performance during the defence of the siege the night before and, in another part, to what the elderly man—Keamard—referred to as the Almber's Glass; the glass with the gold dust embedded in it; Rut had been given a nice room of his own.

It had a four-poster bed, and a large, oak wardrobe—which he had nothing to fill with.

The place was completed with the ceiling-to-floor windows which looked out over the town square, and Rut couldn't help wondering if this was one of the suites which Heffers Tavern reserved for visiting nobility . . . then again, Rut supposed that he was *almost* nobility; he did have a title after all: Rutterness, Royal Guardian of the Waterways.

But news couldn't have spread that fast.

Although it was true that Lou had an admirable network of spies throughout the kingdom, Rut could hardly bring himself to believe that Lou was keeping a day-to-day eye on his own efforts to entice Hildie back to Ilsnare.

After he had spent the best part of the day in his personal quarters, first gorging himself on the honey-roasted pork brought up to him, and then catching up on a great deal of sleep, he was surprised to notice that, while he'd been sleeping, his wardrobe had been fully furnished. And that, within the bathroom, there was a bucket of warm water and soap awaiting him.

He wasted no time in washing himself thoroughly before getting dressed into one of the clean tunics which'd been left for him in the wardrobe.

He chose a downbeat beige tunic and decided to wear it over the top of a pair of light-blue trousers. They were the sort of clothes which Rut would've worn around the house on a well-deserved (to his mind anyway) day off.

Not that he was complaining.

After all that had gone on, after all this distance he had travelled, Rut felt as though he deserved a solid day of doing nothing.

So it was a shame that, following his walk at dusk, through the streets of Nor'tarth, he found the elderly man, Keamard; and his granddaughter, who he'd learned was named Keeva; waiting for him outside his quarters.

Rut noticed, right away, that Keamard was holding the Almber's Glass; that piece of glass with embedded gold dust.

"Good evening," Keamard said, with a warm smile that suggested he really meant it.

Or that he'd had a lot of practice at pretending . . .

"Hello," Rut replied, doing his best to mimic Keamard's—surely false—smile.

Rut turned his attention briefly to Keeva, and took in her straw-blond hair which she had today swept into a neat bun at the back of her head. For some reason, she wore the same purple robes which her grandfather was wearing; and that purple really brought out the beautiful green shade in her eyes.

Keeva smiled at him.

"Everything to your taste?" Keamard asked.

"Yes," Rut replied, "absolutely fine."

Then Rut turned his attention in the direction of the door to his quarters, and he wondered if he was going to be permitted to shift past Keamard . . . although he'd spent most of the day sleeping, he felt as though he could do with another forty winks.

But Keamard stood in his way.

"Listen here, a moment," Keamard replied, flashing a glance over his shoulder at his granddaughter, Keeva. "We were just talking earlier on today and it seems that my granddaughter, here, saw you entering the tavern last night with a little girl." He turned back to face Rut then arched an eyebrow. "Is that correct?"

Rut had never been good at hiding his emotions, and he realised that it would cost him any sort of advantage here.

In the end, assuming that his quick glance away from Keamard had already given up the game, he replied, "Yes, that's right."

Keamard cocked his head to one side. "*Fascinating,*" he said.

Rut again looked past Keamard, once more wondering if he was going to be permitted to pass the elderly man and his granddaughter. He supposed that oft-heard saying, about there never being any such thing as 'free room and board', was very much correct.

"Tell me," Keamard went on, "this girl, wasn't she a member of the Almber?"

Rut looked to Keamard and Keeva. "Yes, that's right—the only one who survived."

Here, Keamard and Keeva exchanged glances.

Keamard gave a nod to Keeva, then he reached out to shake Rut's hand.

He grinned from ear to ear again. "Awfully nice having you to stay here," he said. "I do hope that you'll make yourself comfortable—-any ally of the king is an ally of Nor'tarth."

Rut did his best to smile back in return as he shook Keamard's hand, but he was sure that it came off as being simply a façade. He had never been good at courtly meet-and-greet situations and he was glad that Lou had apparently noticed that for himself.

Once Keamard and Keeva had disappeared from view, Rut took himself back into his room and lay down on the soft bed.

But, no matter how he shifted and turned, he couldn't find any peace and quiet.

His mind, quite simply, wouldn't stop churning away.

Perhaps he would go insane.

30

FRIENDS AMONG FOES

HILDIE SOON LEARNED a great deal about this particular tribe of Horrox.

The large Horrox who had spoken into her mind turned out to be the leader among them. He informed her that his name was Inta. He also informed Hildie that the female Horrox who'd served her the delicious breakfast of porridge was his wife; and called Re'enyi.

What struck Hildie most about the tribe of Horrox was how she was held in a state of near-reverence; how the Horrox would all bow to her before speaking into her mind, asking whether there was anything they might do to 'satisfy her wishes' and she would, as politely as possible, thank them for their concern.

Throughout her days with the Horrox she learned just how high a level of esteem they held her father, Ma'reygar.

Indeed, it was almost as if they had etched his name into their history as some kind of legendary figure.

Many times, Inta invited Hildie to take walks with him, 'inspections' of the encampments, and he would reel through his remembrances of her father and explain more about the Horrox's cause . . . just what it was they wished to achieve and why.

And, as time plodded onward, Hildie couldn't help but feel the spirit of her father still infecting these people; and, perhaps more concerning still, she found herself being whisked away by their ideologies and plans.

Mortals, it seemed, never *dared* to dream this big.

The Horrox, just like all Creatures throughout the kingdom, wanted only one thing:

Freedom.

Her father—Ma'reygar—had always fought for the freedom and equality of Magical beings throughout the kingdom, and that had been one of the principal motivations in waging his magical war. Or, at least, that was what he would have people believe; because Hildie knew that the true reason Ma'reygar had waged war was a personal grudge he had held against Herimyre; Captain of the Royal Guards, and then, later, King of Shellacnass.

As Hildie listened to Inta's arguments surrounding her deceased father, about how he was nothing short of a demi-god, she held the matter firmly in mind that he never would've *dreamed* of raising an army to stand against the Kingdom of Shellacnass if it hadn't been for her mother's death—*his wife*—at the hands of the king and Herimyre.

Her father hadn't been a hero, Hildie had no delusions about that; and, in fact, he had been a long way off in entirely the other direction . . . whichever direction that might've been.

One late-morning, as Hildie was 'inspecting' the encampments with Inta, he took her to one side and—*apparently*—decided to lay out everything in an honest manner.

— *Hilda, you must understand one thing about us.*

Hildie remained still, feeling the cool breeze against her cheeks. The hardy green-brown tunic she had been given by the Horrox helped to guard against the cold; and the fires which were located all about the hillside gave off a delightful collective heat.

She replied to Inta within her own thoughts.

— *What?*

— *We have far more knowledge than you imagine; we are much further embedded in Mortal society than you imagine. You must understand that our cause is not simply one which stands against Mortals themselves, but, indeed, against our own kind.*

Hildie allowed this statement to sink in.

Of course she knew that all sorts of Magical beings had laid low during the times of Herimyre; who had waged a personal war against magic in the kingdom. And, so far as an ordinary Mortal might believe, Herimyre had succeeded in driving every last Magical being over the border of the kingdom, or else into the darkest of corners of the Sable Mountains.

But Hildie had been travelling so long—she had *visited* so many places—that she knew this to be a fallacy. Quite simply put, she knew whenever magic was close by; whether it ran through the veins of some unlikely seeming Mortal . . . a Mortal who, quite often, was a Creature in disguise.

And so it went.

Throughout the kingdom, in the times of Herimyre, and in the times preceding him, it was a known fact, at least throughout the Magical communities, that magic ran deep in the Mortal world;

although its efficacy, of course, depended on a certain façade being maintained, and in said façade never being discovered.

So it didn't seem too large a jump of logic that the Horrox had found their places within Mortal society.

As Hildie turned her attention back to Inta so that she might explain this, she was surprised to find that he was already smiling; apparently having read her thoughts.

She was finding that she had greatly underestimated the telekinetic abilities of the Horrox. They were Creatures, after all, and most likely had been born with the gift. They hadn't needed to practise for lonely hours, building up their base skill until they were confident of trying it out for 'real'.

Inta replied within her own mind once again.

— We are shape shifters, but more talented than the average Creature. What comes with difficulty for Mortals, or for other beings, comes very easily for us. In fact, we can keep up any disguise we wish for years; for decades; as long as our magic isn't called into other areas. As long as we are not forced out of our costumes.

It was here that Hildie took the opportunity to turn her attention back onto Inta.

And when she did she almost fell over backward.

Her heart drummed hard within her chest.

Because, staring back at her, his leathery skin; grasping his old familiar staff with the embedded, worn-down ruts; was her father:

Ma'reygar.

Even as Inta shifted back out of Ma'reygar's form; even as his nose grew long and large out of his reptilian face, Hildie was left with the impression of her dead father smudged across her mind's eye . . . an image she knew, no matter what enchantments she attempted, or which potions she might consume, would never truly be gone.

"How did I do?" Inta said, speaking out loud for the first time, in a strangely perfect Ilsnare dialect.

31
___

WONDERING

A BOUT A WEEK after Inta's brief transformation into
Ma'reygar; Hildie found herself sat on a rock, staring out
over the encampments as a fine rain sprinkled down across the
pitched canvases. It set the entire landscape in a sort of grey-scale
which disoriented her slightly.

She could smell sea salt on the rain—could almost taste it on
the tip of her tongue.

It had always been a difficult task to find her true place in the
real world; and she knew that it would be a struggle until the day
she died.

Was this her place; to take up her father's promises?

To help lead these Creatures to their freedom?

So that, no longer, they would have to lurk in the shadows,
deceiving all those who surrounded them just because it was the
only way they would find acceptance.

Hildie thought about all the 'Mortals' she had met through the years, and all those times when she had felt the magic bubbling just below the surface. She had believed them to be Mortals with a glimmer of magic running through their blood, but, she saw now, they could just as easily have been Creatures keeping themselves concealed so that they might survive.

What if she had breached the subject?

She *had* many times asked imprudent questions whenever she had sensed magic nearby . . . why, Louson Dorf for one . . . and he might well have turned out to be a Creature—and what might've happened then?

He would've been forced to kill her so as to maintain his secret.

To keep on living a lie.

Never having occupied one place for any extended period of time, it seemed an almost alien concept to Hildie. She had never been able to bed down in a community to work out what her real place might be; playacted or not.

It was when this wondering reached its climax, when she caught herself thinking about just what she was meant to be doing in this world, that she stopped dead.

And she realised.

Although she seemed to fit nowhere at all, there were many who wanted her.

Mortals.

The Horrox.

. . . Why?

What was her use to them?

She fancied that if she'd put the question to Rut, he wouldn't have been able to answer. She knew that Lou kept his closest secrets just that way . . . within his own skull.

A most dangerous king.

A most dangerous opponent.

But one thing was for certain.

Lou *did* want her.

And only ten years after they'd parted . . .

Perhaps she should've felt upset about all that time, but the truth of it was that she just felt completely neutral; as if it was nothing more than a fly which had flown into her forehead. She felt it but there was no pain. No anger. Just another insignificant thing that had happened while she kept on moving forward.

While she kept turning in circles.

It was so frustrating whenever she sat back and thought of her life, because, just as her father had told her, she had so much potential within her; so much *Good Breeding* . . . and it was all being 'wasted' in the service of others.

Why should she want to serve at all?

Later on that day, she put the question to Horrox; the question of how they had known to find her; how they had known that she had been located at Almber's Bay.

That same smirk appeared on his lizard lips, and his black eyes seemed to almost open up like a pair of mouths readying to devour her.

He told her that it had been a simple matter of using their 'contacts', the ones who were spread throughout the kingdom and who they communicated with . . . the ones with the finger on the pulse. Through those contacts they had learned that Louson Dorf wished to solicit the services of Hilda and that a close aide of the king had been dispatched to fetch her.

From Almber's Bay.

So it had been Lou all along—Hildie *had* often wondered if she could truly trust him; if he had held to his word, held his promise that he wouldn't come after her. When, all this time, he had been keeping a very close watch on her.

Never allowing her out of his sight.

And yet, Hildie had remained in the kingdom.

Why hadn't she left?

Had she believed that there was a prospect of her being called back?

Did she *wish* him to call her back?

Or had she just wanted to stay close . . . stay close *to him* . . .

Hildie shifted away from Inta before her emotions became too much to handle; before she broadcast too much to the Horrox.

But that did nothing to conceal the truth from herself.

Because, like it or not, there was nothing she could do.

She still loved Lou . . . King Louson, of Shellacnass.

32

THE PROSPECTIVE RAID

IT WAS A SWELTERING DAY when Rut led the guards of Nor'tarth out onto the plains which surrounded the town. Already, he regretted having demanded that every one of them be outfitted in leather armour; along with their regulation swords and range weapons.

It had been a confidence move, of sorts.

Keamard had come to him, declaring that a Royal Messenger had confirmed Rut's relation to the king. With this in mind, Keamard had duly informed him that the mayor had granted Rut the use of whatever resources the town possessed for the completion of his goals.

Rut only had *one* goal.

To bring Hildie back to Ilsnare.

Rut had decided that he needed to look as though he was in control, as if he was the battle-weary veteran that he was surely imagined to be.

At the very least, the people of Nor'tarth knew of his exploits in repelling the Horrox; although Rut was extremely reluctant to claim any sort of credit for the achievement.

He was certain that it had all been down to Hildie.

Convinced.

When the Royal Messenger had arrived to the town, Rut had been of half a mind to send a message back to Lou, declaring that he wasn't the right person for this particular quest; and that Lou had better get someone else.

Rut had even reached the stage where he'd decided that he would claim that this had all got *much bigger* than he had imagined.

He knew that if he had painted a dire enough picture then Lou would've sent great help; a thousand Royal Guards, perhaps . . . and yet Rut had been unable to send the message.

Because he knew that it would be untrue.

Rut was often his worst critic and even though he did the best job of anyone in terms of knocking down his confidence, he knew that he had only to set his mind to the task and he would be able to succeed.

He had journeyed from Ilsnare, all the way here—*singlehanded* —hadn't he?

Even his horse hadn't managed the journey . . .

That had to count for something.

And if it didn't quite inspire confidence in him for the hardy task ahead, then it certainly made him believe that he could give it a good go.

Once Rut stood up before the troops—the two hundred or so that the mayor had turned over to him—he could still feel the eggs from breakfast churning about in his stomach. He had noticed that ever since the Royal Messenger had arrived to town, and confirmed Rut's status, that the quality of his service at the tavern had increased by factors of ten.

And before, it really hadn't been all that bad.

Every morning, Rut woke to a knock at the door and the scent of buttery eggs being brought to him on a silver tray. He would receive the local beverage too; cultivated from beans and known as 'tiway'. That stuff seemed to give him that necessary kick out of bed . . . when the eggs had worked their magic on him and made him slothful.

A man could easily grow accustomed to such luxuries.

And he could just tell that his wife would be *furious* at such a prospect.

Here he was, on this quest, and Rut was supposed to be suffering; he was supposed to be striving for a very noble, extremely significant goal . . . and he had indigestion.

A large glob of sweat rolled down between his shoulder blades. He waited until he felt it trickle all the way down below the waistband of his trousers before he thought it possible to address the troops all spread out before him.

From what Rut had heard from the Nor'tarth spy reports, the location of the Horrox was well known; their encampments were situated on the opposing hillside to the town. When Rut had enquired as to why the forces of Nor'tarth hadn't already struck the stronghold, he had been advised that such an attack slipped into direct contravention with the strategic purpose of the town; which was, as Rut had already witnessed, to be *attacked* and then to launch a *counter-attack*.

Besides, the main complaint had been that the Horrox were

magic practitioners and, as such, needed to be treated with the utmost caution.

Although they had never ventured to do so much in the town, they had already fried a good many caravans passing along the major roads out of Nor'tarth; as if they were proving a point about their superior strength.

As if they had been proving the point that they could easily take the town at a time of their choosing.

Rut could still recall the taut feeling in the air between himself and the garrison representatives. He knew that they were deeply dissatisfied with the situation and, in short, terrified that one day the Horrox *would* decide to obliterate Nor'tarth from the face of the world. And there would be nothing that the garrison would be able to do to stop them.

That was the truth of it.

Although Rut had led troops in the past, he found this to be a much headier prospect. Whereas before it had been his own people he had been marshalling, now he found himself faced with the prospect of leading these people from a faraway land. Despite them speaking in a familiar language, their dialect was strange —*biting almost*—and Rut had to admit that he was still having some trouble coming to terms with it.

Understanding it when it was whispered; or when it was shouted.

Rut put the troops through various drills; the drills which he had envisioned for raiding the Horrox encampments. He could think of no other means of attacking their camp than by going in, under the cover of night, and simply snatching Hildie out from beneath their noses.

And that was assuming a whole lot.

That was assuming that she would come quietly.

That she wouldn't raise up another firestorm, this time directed at Rut.

As Rut maneuvered between the troops of Nor'tarth, he nodded approval and gave grunts of encouragement. He had them crawling about on their bellies, their swords and bows holstered on their backs while they slowly made their way through the long grasses.

Would this be enough to fool the Horrox?

Would the fact that the people of Nor'tarth had never attacked their encampments be enough by way of surprise?

Because the Horrox certainly *wouldn't* expect the attack . . .

Rut spent the rest of the day out on the plains with the troops of Nor'tarth. He couldn't help but feel a glimmer of satisfaction at their preparations. There might be a hope of success yet.

Rut led the troops back into the town, all of them exhausted, their shoulders slumped, and some of them with their heads bowed low to their chests.

He realised that the garrison here—at Nor'tarth—wasn't all that used to physical exertion; and though he realised that it was more likely a case of a strategic decision made higher up the chain of command, Rut couldn't help but think that it was quite a great weakness. He wondered if he should've asked Lou for some Royal Guards after all.

But it was too late now.

Too late for him to send a messenger.

From what he had gathered, the Horrox might chance a final strike on the town of Nor'tarth any day now, and then they would escape Mortal clutches . . . and Hildie would escape Rut's clutches.

And he would've failed.

As Rut led his men through the town streets, he noticed them, first in groups of five or six, and then, one by one, peeling away from him and returning to their homes. He knew that they would all get a good night's sleep; that they would be prepared for the strike which he planned to occur the following night.

That was good.

He *convinced* himself that it was good.

That he was doing all he could.

It was when Rut turned the corner, onto the town square, and approached Heffers Tavern, that he spotted her again.

The little girl.

The little *Almber* girl.

His heart bounced up in his throat.

A chill ran through his blood.

Then he blinked.

And she was gone.

He roamed the streets for the next hour, searching for her high and low, but he knew, no matter how long he looked, he would never be able to track her down.

She slipped through his fingers like a fine sand.

But Hildie would not do the same.

33

NIGHT-TIME THREATS

HILDIE WOKE WITH A START.

Her dreams, as they often were, had been tormented with wicked, twisted faces; with pasty complexions and—above all else—the stench of burning flesh.

To begin with, the encampments were bleary and she had trouble distinguishing the shapes of the tents which surrounded her; even with the torchlight which flickered away over them, never quite casting them in shadow.

She was lying on the bedroll which the Horrox had given her rather than sleeping in one of the tents as the Horrox did. She had chosen to sleep outside, with the stars. She had grown accustomed to doing so after all her travels throughout the kingdom. There seemed something ethereal; something truly *wonderful* about sleeping out under the stars . . . as if she could feel the heavens—and all their infinite possibilities—opening up for her.

Offering her a new life.

A new way of living.

When she shifted slightly, she felt the blade of a knife at her throat.

It cut into her skin.

She could smell the coppery scent of blood.

"Don't you move," came the strained, whispered voice behind her.

Hildie had no intention of moving.

She stayed still.

A bead of warm—*impossibly hot*—blood rolled down her neck.

Hildie faced forward, looking over the rest of the encampments.

Everything so still.

Everything so silent.

On the horizon, she made out Nor'tarth; the steady orange glow of the town at night.

Was this their plan?

To take her off guard during the night?

She might've thought as much . . .

"Stand up," the voice, still at the level of a husky whisper, commanded.

Hildie took her time.

She knew, owing to the benefit of experience, that it was always the safest strategy to do whatever someone with a knife pressed to her throat told her to. She could reconsider the power structure once the blade no longer pressed up against her skin.

Feeling a little unsteady on her feet, she gradually lifted herself up.

Rose up as the voice had told her to.

"Over there," the voice continued.

Although Hildie hadn't much of an idea just where the voice intended her to go, she allowed the hand which clenched the back of her tunic to guide her.

After the first few steps, she could tell that she was being led over to the scattering of trees on the other side of the encampments.

She had often wondered about the Horrox's level of surveillance around their camp—she had never noticed anything so *Mortal* as sentries posted at strategic points. But she supposed that they had a clear idea of what was happening in their immediate surroundings simply by channelling their magic . . . feeling the shifts in the forces around them.

As the voice shoved her on briskly in the direction of the trees, Hildie felt something. A tingle in her veins. A slight sinking of her heart. She had learned to trust these subtle signals; they often told her more than weeks of spying on a person might do.

Magic.

Magic was close by.

Close enough to touch.

As if in response to this query, she felt the voice give her a sharp shove in the back.

Hildie almost stumbled over a stray tree root, sticking up out of the ground.

She caught herself before she plummeted—most likely with the blade of the knife sticking in her throat.

That wouldn't have been anything like the noble, mage's death which her father Ma'reygar had surely dreamed for her ever since she was born.

No, she owed her father's memory much more than to be slain by some cloak-and-dagger in the middle of nowhere.

"Here," the voice said, having brought her to the trees now.

Hildie felt the blade dig deeper into her throat.

More blood trickled down her neck.

Dampened the front of her tunic.

Her heart leaped in her chest.

Perhaps they did plan to kill her.

If they did then she needed to prepare herself.

What was she doing?

If she wished—if she *really* wished—then she could fight back.

She could save her life.

But . . . for what?

The trees were large—*elms?*—and she could hear a faint breeze blowing through the leaves above her head. The grasses swishing about her feet. The voice stood behind her and she could see, from out of the shadows, that another figure lurked.

Her heart skipped several beats.

And her pulse rattled away at her temples.

Slowly but surely, the figure emerged from the shadows.

Out into the moonlight which streamed down through the trees.

It took Hildie several moments to recognise her face, but, when she did, she wondered how she hadn't known who it was all along.

"Let her go," the figure told the voice, still clinging tightly to the back of Hildie's tunic.

The voice sank the blade in a little deeper.

And then relented.

Hildie felt the cool steel retreat from her skin.

And she allowed herself to breathe freely again.

She reached up to her throat, touched the damp, warm blood

which oozed out from the slit. The smell of her own blood covered everything now. It made her want to retch . . . she wondered how she who had killed so many could still be so squeamish . . .

Then she turned her attention back to the figure who'd materialised from the shadows.

That wispy, white beard.

Leathery skin.

The elderly man from Nor'tarth.

Keamard.

And, sure enough, behind her, Hildie spotted his granddaughter.

The voice who'd held the knife to her throat.

The voice, Keamard's granddaughter, spoke. "My name's Keeva," she said. "I don't believe you ever knew it."

34

STIRRINGS IN THE NIGHT

HILDIE FELT as if someone had punched her in the solar plexus.

She wanted to take a few steps backward, as if absorbing a blow.

But she held herself still.

She had to stand here.

And see what it was that they wanted.

What Keamard, and his granddaughter—*Keeva*—wanted from her.

Off, in the direction of the encampments, Hildie sensed stirring.

She knew that Keamard and Keeva didn't have long before the Horrox would surround this outcrop of trees; before their lives would be in grave peril.

From her conversations with Inta, Hildie knew that she was of great value to the Horrox and that they would die to defend her.

This was nothing less than a suicide mission on the part of Keamard and Keeva.

But perhaps that was what they wanted.

"This should be brief," Keamard said, none of the jolliness which'd accompanied his tone present from before. "We have no intention of outstaying our welcome if we are not wanted."

Now that Hildie no longer had the blade of the knife pressed up against her throat, she felt freer to speak her mind. "It's too late," she said, feeling a smirk creep onto her lips. "They're already stirring—already coming to my aid."

Despite this poorly veiled threat, Keamard didn't seem shaken, judging by the sure tone of his voice. "We know who you are, Hilda, daughter of Ma'reygar."

Hildie felt her heart leap a little in her chest.

But she pushed away the feeling.

She turned her attention back to Keamard. "And that doesn't make you want to run—to escape while you still can?"

"The last time I saw Almber's Glass," Keamard replied, apparently unfazed, "was *decades* ago."

Hildie shifted a glance in the direction of Keeva. "Her necklace."

"Yes," Keamard said, "her necklace."

Hildie could see the Almber's Glass hanging off the golden chain about Keeva's neck.

A *tiny* lump compared to the chunk which Hildie had brought with her.

And a drop in the ocean compared to that which she had 'produced' and left behind ...

Her own personal—*beautiful*—trail of destruction.

"I suppose you know where it came from?" Keamard went on; again not sounding in any particular rush.

"Almber's Bay," Hildie replied.

Keamard gave her a wry smile. "Yes, from Almber's Bay," he said, "but *who* produced it?"

Hildie felt wrinkles form in her brow.

She gave a shake of her head.

"I don't know," she said.

This time, instead of Keamard answering, Keeva left her previous position, behind Hildie, and rounded her to stand beside her grandfather. "Don't you see yet?" Keeva replied. "Don't you understand *anything* about your history—about what your father, Ma'reygar, has done?"

"No," Hildie replied, answering honestly.

Where her father was concerned, there were hundreds, if not thousands, of escapades about which she knew nothing.

"That he led the first slaughter of the Almber?" Keeva continued. "That he was the first one to cast the Almber into a firestorm from which they would never escape? That he turned that beach into sheet upon sheet of Almber's Glass?"

Hildie felt her throat constricting, as if the blade was still pressed up against her neck, although she could clearly see that Keeva held the knife down at her side.

Keeva gave Hildie a shrill smile. "I suppose you're glad that you fulfilled the prophecy—that you must have made the old man *proud.*"

The mocking tone stung Hildie, even though she knew that this was nothing but a terrible coincidence. Why, she hadn't set out to destroy the Almber; indeed she had been trying to *protect* them . . .

but magic had overpowered her and made the task an impossible one. And now she would have to suffer the comparisons with her father, although she was certain that she hadn't intended malice.

Had she?

Hildie stared long and hard at the Almber's Glass which hung about Keeva's neck, and, when she spoke again, she surprised herself with her husky, biting tone. "If you're so ashamed of what my father did—of what *I* did—then why do you keep that relic of the genocide so close to your heart?"

Keeva smiled even wider.

Then she reached up and fingered the Almber's Glass.

"Ma'reygar never told you, did he?" Keeva replied.

"Told me what?"

"That he had another woman." Keeva paused for an impossibly long time, and then finally added, "Another *daughter*?"

Hildie felt her heart clench tightly. All the blood rushed to her temples.

Whenever she tried to bring the scene clear before her—to give the twin figures of Keeva and Keamard some sort of a sharper profile—she felt her eyes watering, making the task impossible.

"No," Hildie said, her voice quieter now. "No, he never told me that."

"We only want to know one thing, Hilda," Keamard said. "Where is the little girl—where is the last remaining Almber?"

But already Hildie was shaking her head; both because she didn't know, and because she could see that the Horrox had closed in around them on all sides.

There was nowhere to run.

Keamard and Keeva were as good as dead.

35

THE INVISIBLE AUDIENCE

HILDIE HEARD the snapping of twigs all around.

And she could feel the barely contained *buzz* of magic as it passed through the air.

As it drove the fire in her veins into a kind of frenzy.

Anticipation.

She could feel the sparks tickling at her fingertips, that everything within her was ready to bring her destruction to bear on these two ... on Keeva and Keamard.

Her mind could hardly make sense of what she had been told; that she had a *half-sister* ...

Either unaware of the Horrox who surrounded them on all sides, or not caring at all, Keamard spoke in a low tone. "For the entirety of our lives; the entirety of Keeva's *mother's* life, we dedicated ourselves to conserving the Almber, to keeping them at peace." He shook his head. "And all was going so well until you returned, until you had to shatter their beautiful society."

Perhaps Keamard believed Hildie to be unfeeling; perhaps he truly *did* believe that she had wiped out the Almber in an act of fury . . . but what he couldn't know was how the tears were beginning to prick the corners of her eyes.

But she pushed them down.

Squeezed her eyes shut several times.

Determined to drive the sadness away.

Keamard continued, "All we wish to know is the location of the last surviving Almber, so that we might protect her, so that we might learn what we can from their civilisation before they are wiped from the face of the world."

Hildie felt her chest tighten.

Despite everything these two had said—despite the fact that they had spoken to Hildie as if she was of the same 'evil' cloth as her father—she couldn't help but think that what they said was sincere; that they truly *did* want to protect the Almber . . . or whatever remained of them.

And why should Hildie stand in their way?

There was *no reason* to stand in their way . . . except she had no idea where the little girl might be; she had rushed off into the streets of Nor'tarth without either her or Rut being able to see where she was headed.

And maybe that was for the best.

Perhaps the last surviving member of the Almber could live out her days in happy ignorance; never fully grasping the terrible truth of what had befallen her people.

To Hildie, that sounded like a marvellous life.

If only her own father had taken the decision to keep her ignorant of the blood which ran through her veins . . .

On all sides now, out in the darkness, Hildie could sense the

Horrox.

They were creeping closer every second.

Their razor-sharp claws down at their sides; ready to bring them to bear on these invaders.

Hildie sensed movement from Keeva, and she shifted a glance in her direction.

Keeva had brought the knife up to her chest.

Although her grip was tightened about the handle, Hildie could see that Keeva was shaking violently; that she, if her grandfather did not, sensed the danger lurking just beyond the trees.

"*Murderer!*" she cried out. "Senseless—*idiotic*—destroyer!"

And with those final words, Keeva launched herself forward, the blade of the knife whipping back in her hand, ready to be brought down into Hildie's skull.

Hildie stood her ground.

She knew that this was her time.

That now she just needed to hold still.

To accept death.

It had been a long time in coming . . .

She waited.

And waited.

Waited still longer.

But she never felt the pain.

The tearing, searing-hot sensation of the knife slipping through her flesh.

Perhaps this was death.

Was she in the heavens now?

Or . . . somewhere else . . .

Finally, Hildie thought to open her eyes.

Did she imagine clouds, lightness—*the sun?*

Or did she believe that she would see only the rising flames; leaping up so that they might encompass her heart: lock it down forever in an obsidian dungeon?

Keeva lay at Hildie's feet.

Dead.

Lifeless, glassy eyes.

The same green eyes as Hildie.

The same green eyes of her father.

Ma'reygar.

But Hildie hadn't been the one to kill her.

Her magic had remained in her veins.

She stood back.

Saw the Horrox crouched down over Keeva's prostrate body.

Its claw sticking into her neck.

Blood still pumping from the wound.

Slowly, the Horrox turned its head up to Hildie.

To meet her eyes with its oily black irises.

It was Inta.

He spoke into her mind.

— *Return to the encampments. We shall deal with the bodies.*

For a dizzy few moments, Hildie thought he had made some mistake. There was only one body. There was only *Keeva's* body ... but then her gaze widened to encompass the elderly man —*Keamard*—on his knees, a pair of Horrox having run him through with their own claws.

It had been a grisly, but silent, attack.

Above all else, though, Hildie knew one thing.

That Keeva and Keamard had come to her here, tonight, unafraid to die for what they believed in. It seemed such a waste that they had been foolish in their *belief* that Hildie had any idea at all about where the little girl—about where the last surviving member of the Almber—truly was.

Inta spoke within her mind again.

— *Go. Take some rest. We have much to speak about in the morning.*

Hildie continued to stare at the pair of bodies which lay before her, and then, feeling a heaviness in her heart which she had previously never experienced, she turned away.

And returned to the encampments.

36

DOUBTS AND MURDER

R UT COULD STILL HEAR the banging reverberating around his head as he shifted himself down the staircase of Heffers Tavern. He had been woken by a violent *thud-thud-thud* of a fist on the door of his quarters, and it'd taken all the strength he possessed not to grab one of the—*expensive-looking*—porcelain lamps and toss it at the wall.

He was glad that he hadn't, although he was near certain that this kind of behaviour was only what was expected from anyone tied up with the nobility.

He worked to button his shirt-coat over his stomach, which had begun to grow back out into its familiar shape during the days he'd spent in Nor'tarth.

From down below, from the kitchens of the tavern, he could smell the delicious scent of onions, eggs and ham. He would have loved to indulge himself in a little breakfast, although the visitor who'd awaited him at the door hadn't allowed him the privilege.

No, his presence was required *at once*!

He had given his troops the entire day off so that they would have a chance to rest up before the raid took place later that night; and he hadn't expected to be disturbed until night-time at the earliest . . . so this was *greatly* frustrating.

Arriving on the ground floor of the tavern, he fixed his stare to the back of the manservant's heels. He could tell that the boy wasn't much more than seven or eight summers old. In many ways, the manservant reminded Rut of himself at that age; with a thatch of blond hair and a rumbling gut which always seemed to expose a half moon of creamy flesh. One thing was for certain, the boy had a *particularly* heavy fist.

By the time they'd crossed the town square, Rut was already out of breath and feeling the hunks of beef he'd chomped down on the night before rising up at the back of his throat. It had been impossible to resist the spiced meat, and all the delicious, tomato-flavoured garnish which'd gone with it. Each time a servant had arrived at the table, Rut had felt it *rude* to turn down the offer.

And he was going to suffer for it now . . .

As he left the town square behind, following closely on the manservant's heels, he couldn't help but cast his mind back to the night when the Horrox had arrived to the town; when they had come to take Hildie away.

In his mind's eye, he could still see their bodies piled up on the cobblestones as the unmerciful arrows and crossbow bolts took them down.

As the various projectiles passed through their heads and their hearts.

Although Rut hadn't the breath to ask the boy where they were headed, it turned out to be unnecessary seeing as they arrived outside a sturdy-looking, pit-black door with reinforced iron keeping it nice and shut from the outside world.

He glanced to the boy whose only response was to reach up for the big, dull brass knocker and to bring it down with a series of hefty *clunks*.

No wonder the boy had succeeded in getting Rut out of bed.

He supposed the boy would have no trouble raising the dead if he really had to.

A matter of seconds later, and after a brief kerfuffle from within, the door opened in on itself to present a sober-looking man with a pale complexion. The man wore something like a butcher's apron tied about his waist. A strange scent of rotting emanated from within the building and Rut felt as if he might trip over his feet and land with a *thump* on the cobblestones beneath him.

But he held on.

Already he could tell what that smell represented.

Death.

"You are the representative of the Crown?" the man asked, his voice smooth and deliberate, and yet, all at the same time, it sent a shudder down the back of Rut's collar.

There was something *distasteful* about the man, but, then again, he supposed that one who chose to live out his existence with the dead could hardly be expected to be a barrel of laughs . . .

"That's right," Rut replied.

The man nodded. "This way, please."

Rut glanced to the manservant, expecting that he might've made himself scarce, but, on the contrary, he was peering with unchecked interest into the gloomy corridors; staring off after the man who had disappeared.

The mortician.

Despite Rut's best efforts, throughout his life, to avoid mortuaries, he'd found himself in more than half a dozen of them over the years.

And this was another for him to mark down on the mental list.

As his eyes streamed with tears from the smell, as he felt the smell seeping through his skin and getting into his very bones, he somehow managed to note the fine, ceramic tiles which covered the place from ceiling to floor; and then the mournful—somehow *appropriate*—pillars which hung down to support the roof of the building.

When he followed the mortician, turning the corner into the principal chamber, Rut brought the collar of his shirt up to cover his mouth and nostrils. He couldn't believe that the mortician himself had no such troubles. That he could quite casually walk about the mortuary without, apparently, suffering any ill effects.

When Rut took in the principal chamber, he found himself faced with a series of stone tables; all laid out in a row.

Torchlight illuminated the room.

Only two of the ten or so tables were occupied with bodies, and those bodies were stripped naked with nothing but a shroud to cover the most intimate parts.

Through bleary eyes, Rut flashed a glance at the mortician, and then looked back at the manservant who'd followed him in. The manservant, just as he was, struggled with the stench of death and decay which clung to the place; and he too had brought the collar of his shirt up to cover his airways.

If the manservant had been his daughter then it would've been a simple task of Rut telling her to go outside—to not come in and see these sights.

To smell these *smells*.

But since Rut had no relationship with the boy at all, it wasn't his place to say whether he should stay or go . . . for all Rut knew, the boy was a spy sent by Lou to keep an eye on him—to make sure that Rut *was* indeed making a valiant effort at tracking down Hildie and bringing her back to Ilsnare.

The mortician approached the first of the stone tables, and Rut felt the beef from the night before stir in his stomach. He couldn't guarantee that he'd be able to hold himself back; that he'd be able to hold onto his most natural of reactions to this most *unnatural* of sights.

As Rut drew closer, he saw that the body occupying the table, lying flat on its back, was that of an old man . . . it took him another second to twig that this was Keamard; the elderly man who had bothered him at the door of his quarters more times than he could count, wanting to know about the location of the little girl, the last surviving member of the Almber.

Perhaps, if Rut had thought to remember it, he could've informed Keamard that he'd seen the little girl skittering about the streets; alone, but apparently content.

But now Rut wouldn't get a chance.

Because Keamard was here—*dead.*

Although Rut wasn't anywhere near being a fanatic of mortuaries, he had to admit that, after the first couple of times he'd stepped inside them, that the effect of the dead had worn off. That was to say that the *sight* of them had worn off; the *smell* continued to be just as abhorrent as ever. He slipped the mortician another glance and wondered just how he could cope with the stench day in and day out.

Surely *nobody* could become accustomed to a smell like this.

He eyed the corpse of Keamard.

The mortician apparently decided this was his moment to speak up.

"Left just outside the town—spotted at first light." The mortician indicated with his bare fingers the chest of Keamard's corpse. "As you can see, the claws entered through the ribcage—*penetrated* the heart."

Although the mortician's tone was flat, his voice almost devoid of emotion, Rut picked up that little hop when he described the more grisly details.

Rut turned his attention down to the stone guttering which ran around the body, and which, he could see, was collecting all the liquids streaming out of it through clinically precise holes in the appendage.

The guttering mechanism made a low, barely perceptible *gargling* sound.

And it made the hair on the back of Rut's neck rise up.

"Death would have been instantaneous," the mortician continued, drawing his hand away from the corpse, and then trudging to the other stone table, on top of which lay the other body.

Rut gave Keamard a final glance and then took the mortician's movements as his cue to shift his attention to the next body.

Keeva . . . Keamard's granddaughter.

"In this case," the mortician drawled on, "the victim was penetrated by claws through the neck and throat." He paused for a second, apparently to allow the image to build in Rut's mind, and then he added, "She would've *choked* on her own blood, I would imagine."

Rut stared long and hard at the straw-blond hair, and then the glassy, wide-open eyes:

Green, just like Hildie's.

He felt a knot twist in his throat.

Then he turned away.

When he dared a glance back at the mortician, he saw that he'd begun to cover Keeva's body with the shroud. He noticed, too, that the mortician wore a wry smile at the corner of his mouth. He had no doubt that the mortician had enjoyed this . . . that he had enjoyed his reaction to the sight.

That aside, Rut had a question lingering on his mind. "The Horrox?" he said.

The mortician finished covering Keamard's body and then glanced up.

He gave Rut a dour nod.

Rut turned back to the manservant, who had gone a rather grim, green-white shade. All the muscles in Rut's body clenched tight. When he spoke again, he addressed the mortician. "Why did you show me this—why was this so *urgent*?"

The mortician stared down into his hands as he rubbed them together. He gave a pout and then mumbled away a reply almost too quiet for him to make out. "Although it's not my place, I do believe that the mayor intended that you understand what it is you're up against." The mortician glanced up from his hands. "So that you make no mistake as to how *foul* these beasts are." His voice grew crisper, and a touch louder, as he added, "And how all those who associate with them should be brought to justice equally and without prejudice."

Rut stared at the now-shrouded stone tables, and the shapes of the corpses which lay beneath the wretched coverings. And then he turned back to the manservant, put his arm about the boy's shoulder and said, "Come on, let's go get you some broth—it'll warm you up."

As Rut turned his back on the mortician, he could feel the boy shuddering as he held him. One thing *was* for certain; these really were *foul* beasts . . . and if Hildie had anything at *all* to do with them, there was no doubt in Rut's mind that she, too, should be left out in the wilderness.

Her power, it was true, would be an asset.

But at what cost?

37

A DREARY DAY

HILDIE HAD WOKEN THAT MORNING to feel a chilly, almost ice-cold drizzle falling over her. She had been sleeping outside, of course—as she preferred it—and she had had to take cover beneath a nearby tree.

As she had stood with her back pressed up against the bark, staring down over the grisly grey landscape; the constantly falling silver rain, she had found herself fixing her attention on Nor'tarth and wondering at the warmth the gleaming torchlights might bring to her blood.

But she hadn't wondered too long, because, make no mistake, there was no turning back.

She knew now that the Horrox had delivered the bodies of Keamard and Keeva to the town that they would be actively after her; that she had last been seen to wander among them, apparently without coming to harm.

She would be an enemy like any other.

What were her options now?

She knew the Horrox would inevitably plan on knocking over Nor'tarth, taking the settlement under their control—if only to show their strength—but where was her place in that?

How did they envision *her* role?

Had they scouted her out at Almber's Bay, sacrificed their own kind, simply so that they might see her power for themselves?

Know that *she* was the weapon they'd been waiting for.

The one which could reduce Mortal towns and villages to ashes.

Perhaps—if she put her mind to it—she could even reduce Ilsnare itself to cinders.

That was what Inta had informed her, but was he really to be trusted?

What might he say if he found out that she—*Hilda*—didn't share the same, extreme views which her father had . . . the ones which'd led him to waging a magical war?

Would the Horrox turn on her?

Destroy her?

She had no way of knowing.

As Hildie observed the drizzle tumbling down over the long grasses, she turned her attention back to the copse where she had met with Keamard and Keeva the night before . . . where she had seen the Horrox murder them.

At first she believed she had something in her eye—that a fly had perhaps flown right into her eyeball. Or that her brain might be playing tricks on her; replaying the scene which'd unfolded.

A scene which, she knew, she would never forget.

But, Hildie was certain, she could see a silhouette there, among the trees.

With a quick glance back to the encampment, she saw that none of the Horrox had yet risen from their slumber. Even as she padded swiftly through the long grasses, feeling the dew dampen the legs of her trousers, she already knew what a dim-witted thought *that* was . . . that the Horrox, unlike her—unlike *Mortals*—depended far more on magical fields than on sight. That was how they had known Keamard and Keeva had arrived at the encampments.

She would need to be speedy.

She couldn't waste time.

Whoever this was who'd come to meet her, she was certain that they must've travelled from Nor'tarth. Since they'd come on foot, they must've left the town at first light—or just before.

Most likely they'd set off before they'd found out that Keamard and Keeva had been murdered by the Horrox last night.

As Hildie got closer to the trees, breathing in the sweet, vibrant smell of rain clinging to the grass, and to the leaves, she wondered if it might be Rut.

It *would* be just like him to try something so reckless.

For him to stride out of Nor'tarth to meet with her; believing himself immune from danger.

Well, he might've got lucky at times in the past—and more so when Lou was close to him—but, if he didn't scarper at haste from here, before the Horrox stirred, then he might just find that his luck had run out.

However, as Hildie closed the gap on the copse, she soon saw that it couldn't be Rut.

For one, the body shape was all wrong.

No *roundness* to it.

Just straight up and down.

Skinny.

Small.

And then it struck Hildie.

Just who it was.

The little girl.

The last of the Almber.

38

SINGULAR HOPE

O N INSTINCT, Hildie glanced back over her shoulder.

She nearly convinced herself that there would be a whole legion of Horrox standing there, ready to form a semi-circle about the copse.

As she had already seen, they were merciless when they faced off with those weaker than themselves; when they truly *wanted* to win a victory.

Last night, in order to kill Keamard and Keeva, they hadn't even bothered to use magic.

Their claws had been more than sufficient to ensure rapid deaths.

What might the Horrox think if they discovered one of the Almber had survived?

Hildie trod closer to the girl, already deeply aware that she might disappear at any moment; as she had done so back in the town.

As she got closer to her, as she took in her squashed nose, her dark features, Hildie couldn't help but give a slight smile. It was reassuring to see that the little girl was safe and sound; that she hadn't succumbed to any of the dangers of the plains.

And then, soon after that glimmer of hope, Hildie felt a crushing weight take over.

Because there was nothing more that Hildie could do to help her.

The girl must return—*alone*—to Nor'tarth.

The same way she'd come.

Before Hildie could utter a word, the little girl spoke to her.

She spoke to Hildie just as the Horrox did.

Within her *mind* . . .

— *My people died to protect you.*

Hildie found herself speechless; unable even to imagine the words into her own mind.

She glanced around again, certain once more that the Horrox had come to finish off the job that they had started . . . the massacre of the Almber.

Hildie scrabbled for the words, and then placed them in the little girl's receptive mind.

— *I was trying to protect* them; *to keep the Horrox away.*

The little girl stared back with her mournful, hazel-brown eyes.

— *The Horrox never would have come if it hadn't been for your presence among my people. You were the reason for their slaughter. Just like your father.*

Hildie found herself lost for several moments.

She was strangely trapped between laughing and crying.

Perhaps she should've done both.

How did this little girl—*no more than eight summers old*—know anything at all about her father?

About Ma'reygar?

Had her father somehow become such a cautionary tale, of how he had brought into existence Almber's Glass, that the parents and grandparents had relayed it to their children?

And how did this little girl tie *her* to her father?

As far as Hildie could recall, she had never heard so much as an uttering about her family.

Much less about her *father.*

And yet, there it was.

Hildie decided to turn the conversation around; to put the emphasis back on this little girl who, apparently, knew so much about her.

— *Why did my father commit the slaughter? Why did he choose to destroy your people?*

The little girl stayed very still; her eyes hardly moving in their sockets.

And then she replied into Hildie's mind once more.

— *Because we wouldn't join with him; we wouldn't acquiesce to his desires.*

— *Such as?*

— *For us to join with him; to become his allies in brewing war. And so, in his anger, he turned his magic upon my people; and he wiped them away.*

Hildie thought that this squared up with her father's penchant for losing his temper.

If there was anything her father hated above all else, it was being told that he couldn't have something; especially when someone—*usually himself*—had promised that particular thing to him.

The little girl continued:

— *My people have a strong affinity with the sea. Your father, he wished for us to use our relationship with the maritime Creatures to help him build his army. So that he might be able to control the seas. That way he hoped to control the whole of Shellacnass.*

Again, Hildie found herself wondering at the megalomania of her father.

And yet, at the same time, she felt a certain sadness.

Because he *had* been her father.

She would never have another.

But Hildie decided to pick up on one point:

— *And so, your people, they took me in knowing full well who I was?*

Here the little girl smirked slightly—a gesture which seemed to be much older than her apparent age. Then she replied:

— *Why else do you think you were allowed to live? My people are forgiving; always willing to give those who have been past aggressors, who are related to past aggressors, another chance. But, do not worry, it is not a mistake we shall make again.*

Hildie felt as if somebody had hollowed out her chest.

And, all at the same time, she felt a slight tickle within her veins.

The knowledge that there *weren't* any Almber to commit to that threat of vengeance. The fact that they wouldn't have stood a chance against her might was secondary.

But Hildie didn't think to press upon it.

This little girl, she had to be suffering from trauma.

She might *never* quite realise the truth.

Hildie turned back to the little girl, fixed her with a stare and then said:

— *What happens next?*

The little girl stared back into Hildie's eyes, and, without another word, disappeared into thin air.

39

PREPARATIONS FOR A NIGHT-TIME CHARGE

RUT COULD FEEL his whole body racked with tension.

All day, the only thing he had managed was a small snack consisting of bread and cheese. It had been just enough to settle his stomach. To keep him from feeling that his skull might split open from the constant hammering of his heart.

The day was coming to an end, and the sound of men working at their weapons—making sure blades were sharp; that all mechanisms were well lubricated—sounded on all sides. He could also hear the stirrings of the horses as their handlers got them ready.

It was strange how many things animals could perceive.

Sometimes Rut wondered if they might be able to perceive things which mere Mortals hadn't a chance of perceiving.

Down in one of the paddocks of the garrison, Rut worked to clean his own weapons: his crossbow and his broad sword. Secretly, he hoped he would need to use neither.

But, in reality, having experienced the terror which the Horrox had brought upon Almber's Bay, he knew that was a fantasy. In fact, it was unlikely that a single one of them would return from this evening's skirmish.

Throughout the day, Rut had been unable to find any sleep in his quarters.

What the mortician had informed him had been true. At his tavern room door, he had met with a succession of representatives of Nor'tarth, all of them not-so-subtly pushing him in the direction of extracting revenge from the Horrox for the atrocities they'd committed the night before.

Rut knew this tactic well, that the Horrox had deigned to leave the bodies of Keamard and Keeva on the principal road to Nor'-tarth precisely so that the early-rising merchants would be the first to see them . . . and by breakfast time ensure the news had spread throughout town.

And it had worked a treat.

He thought about how, when they had first arrived to Nor'-tarth, everyone had seemed so relaxed; so at *ease*. He wondered if this had been due to a sense of false confidence; that their town could easily repel any strike forced against it.

He couldn't help wondering if, when the Horrox had come before, they had been willing to allow their numbers to be picked off by the archers and the crossbowmen concealed in the upper reaches of the townhouses so that they might breed a false sense of security.

They had only attacked with anything like their full numbers —and certainly *not* with their full strength—when they had realised Hildie was concealed within the town.

Although the conversations Rut had had with the spies of Nor'tarth had suggested to him that they *understood* that the

Horrox possessed magical powers, they didn't *truly* understand the extent of that power; that, if they so wished it, they could crush Nor'tarth as if it were nothing but an ant hill beneath their boot heels.

And the ants would all rush around.

Search for their partner.

Stay close.

Await death.

Rut channelled his attention back into the weapons lying on the stone workbench before him. He breathed in the strong, slimy scent of the oil he used to keep the mechanism of his crossbow sleek and smooth.

He tested the trigger several times.

Felt the *twang* of the sprung wire flinging free.

It was all like being a skuller:

The running around at night.

Firing off shots at a Magical menace which—in reality—could never be tamed by Mortal weapons.

This time, though, many more of them would die.

And it wouldn't be just a sprinkling of men all dressed in black.

Ones who no one would miss.

This time it would be a *slaughter*.

But, as Rut looked about the faces of his troops, he knew there was nothing he could do to stop it.

Some of them were smiling.

So *completely* unaware of the fate which awaited them.

Why, by morning, he fancied every last one of them would be lying on the plains, their guts opened to the sunrise.

Right as Rut felt his hands begin to shake, as the enormity of what was about to pass hit home, he felt as if somebody was watching him.

From the shadows.

He turned to look.

And there he saw her.

Once more.

The little girl.

He looked about himself once more, to see if one of the soldiers might've seen her too, but none of them looked in her direction.

Feeling his pulse rise up to his temples, he approached.

Away from the chattering of troops preparing for battle, Rut felt an odd calm descend.

The little girl exerted something over him.

Perhaps she played on his fatherly sensibilities; reminding him of his wife and own little girl back home.

He could hardly believe that he might never see them again.

But he had to make peace with that fact before battle.

Otherwise fear might turn him into a coward.

His heart beat against his ribcage, and it felt as if invisible hands clung tightly to his throat. Whenever he strained his eyes to see into the darkness, to better see the little girl's face, he felt as if he was sinking deeper into the ground; as if some strange force had a claim on him and was determined to drag him under.

But he held himself steady.

And kept his muscles as relaxed as he could.

The paddocks of the garrison were designed so that there were many stone tables for the troops to prepare their weapons, just as Rut had been doing. Each table was kept divided from the other by a small wall. Not much to offer by way of privacy, but it proved just enough to keep the little girl shielded from careless glances.

Rut could smell the brutal odour of horse flesh slice through the night; that stench which got right to the back of his throat, and which seemed to sink into the pores of his skin.

He looked to the little girl and he waited.

She was the one who had come here—to see *him*.

As she had done before, she spoke directly into his mind.

— *I have come to say goodbye, and to wish you luck.*

Not wanting to speak aloud and be thought mad by those who overheard him conversing with a brick wall, he gave a slight smile and a firm nod.

The little girl smiled back at him.

— *The goodness of Mortals often catches me off guard; as much as the capacity of magic to do evil. It catches us all off guard.*

Rut thought he could relate to this, and he wondered if there would ever come a time when cruelty would be completely smothered from the world.

Finally, Rut shrugged off his inhibitions and spoke.

"Where will you go?"

Despite having spoken aloud, the girl answered within his mind:

— *Home.*

Rut thought about the obvious question; he thought to put to her the fact that she no longer had a home . . . at least not at Almber's Bay.

That life was gone.

Those *people* were gone.

But just who did he think he was to stamp all over this little girl's happiness?

All over these *coping* mechanisms she'd developed to ease her grief?

So Rut simply gave her a smile, and said, "Take care."

Just like that, as subtly as she had arrived, she slipped away into the air.

Into the shadows.

When Rut returned to tend his weapons, he was surprised to find that his hands had ceased shaking. His heart had regained its familiar, relaxed rhythm.

If this was to be his last day on Earth then he would do his best.

His *very* best.

Nobody would *ever* be rightly able to call him a coward.

40

OUR FLAGBEARER

B Y THE TIME Hildie returned to the encampments from the copse, after taking a long walk following her meeting with the little girl, the sun had come out.

And she could feel the fire magic prickling about her veins.

She almost felt as if she had snapped back into something like normality.

The succulent smells of brewing porridge filled the air; that rich scent of oats mixed up with honey and other condiments which Hildie couldn't name.

From within the tents, the Horrox were emerging, poking their heads out.

Many of them had been asleep; having a nap.

Hildie wondered what they might believe lay ahead, what they might expect from having her on their side.

Did they expect that new levels of destruction—of *firepower*— were within their grasp?

She could say one thing with outright certainty, and it was that if they required a leader they would be much better served to find one among themselves.

Among the Horrox.

Inta, as far as Hildie could tell, was quite suitable.

He seemed to share the passion of leaders.

A passion which Hildie, in truth, would never quite be able to muster.

As for her, all she wanted was a little peace and quiet.

And if those things came with freedom and equality for all Magical beings, then so be it.

Once Hildie had had breakfast, and felt as if she might never be hungry again, she headed on off for the nearby stream where she bathed herself; where she put on the clothes which the Horrox had provided for her.

It was strange to think that she had had a sister.

She wondered if—*in truth*—her father had ever known about her.

She supposed that he had made himself scarce once he had wiped out the Almber; that he had headed off for pastures new.

Leaving behind a woman bearing his child.

When Hildie returned to her sleeping spot, she lay down on her leather bedroll and thought about taking a brief nap. It seemed as though the past few days had knocked a huge amount of energy out of her. She just needed some time to drift away.

To cut herself free.

But it seemed that time would have to wait.

Because she could already see Inta approaching.

He arched his broad, muscular shoulders; and, as was the case with all of the Horrox, he wore nothing on his torso, and only a pair of ragged trousers beneath. She took in the scabbed, red-raw skin and the horned protrusions in his skull.

Although she hadn't had a large amount of interaction with Creatures in her youth, her father, Ma'reygar, had always taught her that they were nothing to be afraid of . . . that—just as with everything else which made up nature—they were part of some divine fabric.

Here for a purpose.

For what purpose, her father could never say.

The gods?

For the heavens?

Hildie liked to think that they had simply come to be as part of the great natural variation; and just as there were dwarfs, or elves, or cyclops—countless other Creatures—there were the Horrox.

Why any living being—'Creature' or 'Mortal'—chose to define or exclude another really seemed beyond Hildie's comprehension.

And, more to the point, it seemed almost an exercise in futility.

Because, as Inta had explained to her, those who were kept to the periphery of society would often find their way into the inner circle through virtue of *vengeance*.

She, the daughter of Ma'reygar, should've known the power of that 'virtue' better than anyone.

Inta gave her a slight smile as he approached. It crossed the lips of his lizard-like snout. His inky-black eyes fixed onto hers. And she waited for the words to enter her mind directly:

— *How are you feeling?*

She held herself still and surveyed the plains.

She stared long and hard at Nor'tarth and wondered what Rut might be doing right at that moment.

Was he even still there, or had he begged his leave off Lou via some Royal Messenger?

. . . No, she was certain that she could almost *reach out* and feel him close by.

And, no matter how much he might look a coward, she knew that nothing could be further from the truth; that he was more valiant than he appeared.

Just to think about how he had volunteered himself for the defence of the town; that he had taken up a crossbow and done his best to ward off the invaders . . . until Hildie had snapped to her senses and realised that it was *her* they wanted.

She turned her attention back to Inta, realising that he had asked her a question.

— *I'm fine.*

Inta inclined his head slightly, in a nod, then sat down before her on the ground; again cross-legged.

— *So, Hilda, you've had time to think about it; to think about your role, about our proposition. What do you say?*

Her heart bounced.

The fire from her magic burned hard about her veins.

She thought about what the Horrox were proposing; what they wanted from her.

Was she clear on what they wanted from her, or had she just assumed?

She turned her attention back to Inta.

Then spoke into his mind:

— *Do you intend to raze Nor'tarth?*

Inta remained where he was, legs still crossed, his palms now resting on the red-raw skin of his kneecaps. He replied to her:

— *That depends.*

— *Depends on what?*

— *On your answer.*

Hildie stared back into those pit-black eyes.

She recalled how, among Mortals, one of the liveliest moral topics was on the subject of whether or not Creatures had a soul.

She wondered to herself how many of those Mortals involved in those discussions had actually knowingly sat down and stared into the eyes of a Creature opposite them.

Probably a handful.

Far more would've, unknowingly, had conversations with Creatures disguising themselves; whether it was through a potion, or through some more subtle—*intrinsic*—means like the Horrox and their shapeshifting.

Inta continued:

— *This morning we sent the bodies to the town. We left them where anybody could see them. We expect an attack to come at nightfall; anything else would be to lose face. To give in to the terror which lurks on the periphery.*

Hildie couldn't help but butt in with her reply:

— *It'll be a massacre. Even without me you'll cause carnage. You won't leave a single one of their soldiers standing.*

— *Yes, I imagine so.*

Hildie's mind went woozy.

She couldn't quite get her head around the matter-of-fact tone.

She wondered if Mortal lives—if other *Creatures'* lives—were anything but a numberless bunch of ants to the Horrox.

Or perhaps they had simply suffered at the hands of Mortals so long that they cared no more.

Perhaps they had been so patient that their rage had built into an unsurpassable tide.

Ready to come crushing down.

Then Hildie thought of what she might do herself.

She replied to him:

— *How can I prevent this from happening? How can I prevent needless deaths?*

— *Do you choose to join with us?*

— *You make it sound as though I can leave you; without any conse-quences. As if I can simply cut the rope and cast myself free.*

— *Nobody can tie up a mage. It's an impossibility.*

Hildie analysed Inta's final words and wondered if there was truth behind them.

Might it be that she *really could* still escape from all this?

This time it would be a clean break.

Away from Shellacnass.

Away from Louson Dorf.

Forever.

She turned back once more to Inta, wanting to clarify.

— *So, if I join with the Horrox, you will spare the people of Nor'-tarth? But, if I don't, if I choose to run away, you will raze the town. And then many others.*

Inta remained quiet for a long time; pensive.

Without warning, he reached down into his trouser pocket and produced something from within. When Hildie finally got a good look at it, she realised that it was the Almber's Glass which Keeva had worn on a golden chain around her neck.

Inta said nothing as he held out the Almber's Glass, dangling at the end of its golden chain.

At first, Hildie was certain she wouldn't take it from him.

She felt the repulsion almost open up within her guts; every-thing forcing her away from this grim keepsake. But then, feeling a tingle of fire through her blood, she reached for the pendant which Inta held out to her.

She took it from him.

Clasped it in her fist.

They sat in silence for the longest time; neither of them even speaking into one another's mind.

The two of them, at least the way Hildie saw it, enjoying the gentle caress of the warming, tropical breeze.

Finally, as if a bell had chimed to announce the end of this meeting, Inta straightened up, rose to his feet, and spoke his parting words into her mind:

— *You have until twilight. You can stay, or you can go. That is the decision you must make.*

As Hildie watched Inta slip away, lose himself among the encampments, the other Horrox sunning themselves on the hillside, she felt more confused than ever.

And yet, at the back of her mind, there was a flicker of hope.

That this time—*finally*—she could get away.

41

MARCH ON THE ENCAMPMENTS

S ADDLED ON HORSEBACK, Rut had to admit that he felt somewhat puffed-up to be leading the troops of Nor'tarth toward the encampments of the Horrox.

He wondered how the rank-and-file soldiers must feel; in their leather armour, with their weapons ready to be drawn.

Did they truly believe that there was any hope at all of victory?

When Rut cast glances over their number, he noted that they all seemed to share the same expression of optimism; and he could only gather that they *did* think this was a battle they could win.

They had ventured forth from Nor'tarth as soon as the night had rolled in, and Rut could still recall the feeling as they had made their procession through the streets of the town.

How the townspeople had all stood in the doorways of their homes, many of them with candles and torches in their hands, lighting their way through the deserted cobblestone streets.

In his mind, Rut could still hear the sharp *chipping* tones of the horses' hooves as they rebounded off the cobblestones, and the cries of encouragement from the townspeople following them for miles beyond the boundaries of Nor'tarth.

Once they had left the town behind, the brisk, pleasantly warm, night-time wind had blown in over the plains.

Already, Rut could feel himself sweating beneath his leather armour.

He squeezed his horse's flanks with his thighs, easing his men forward, occupying his position at the front of the column.

Soon enough, they would break apart, and start into their plan.

The idea was for them to attack the encampments on all sides.

For them to commit to a sneak-attack.

One group of troops popping up on each side—swords drawn, crossbow bolts and arrows arcing through the air and into the accumulated sleeping Horrox.

No mercy.

But, for the time being, they would remain together— venturing forth as one.

Already Rut knew that this was a tactical mistake, that the Horrox would have scouts—or whatever method they employed to keep an eye on their surroundings—and the troops all grouped together would only mean that they were easier to spot.

Easier to group together and *kill.*

Rut supposed, by some fatalistic logic, that he would prefer the deaths of his troops to come close to home; so that the Death Carts wouldn't have far to return the fallen soldiers to their loved ones.

He almost *wished* the attack would come now.

That the anticipation would be over.

Finally.

But, as his horse plodded on, still leading the column, the realisation dawned on him that there was not yet any end in sight.

That they might yet have a bloodily fought battle ahead.

Rut kept in mind the plan as they reached the first waypoint—a simple milestone, overgrown with long grasses—which'd been pointed out to him by the spies of Nor'tarth as an appropriate point for him to break the column.

So that they might go their separate ways.

And surround the enemy.

He brought his horse to an abrupt halt at the milestone and turned to gaze over the assembled troops.

And then he turned to look to the horizon.

He'd been hoping.

Truly hoping.

Perhaps now . . . yes, maybe it would be *right now* that the hexes would begin to fly through the air; that the Horrox would reveal themselves to be lurking on all sides.

Ready to attack.

But nothing happened.

Rut sat silent on the back of his horse as his deputies barked orders to the troops, detailing which paths they should follow.

Rut, himself, had made it so that he would lead the northern group.

So that he would be the one to head up the troops attacking the encampments head on.

He could still recall the impressed looks on the faces of those among the Nor'tarth administration; how they had thought this to be Rut's grandest statement of reckless bravery. But nothing could be further from the truth.

Rut's only hope now was that he might be among the first to die.

Then, maybe, this killing would have all come to an end by the time he woke in the heavens.

With nothing else to be done, he allowed the splitting of the column to take place, and his inferiors led off their own groups of troops, headed for the encampments where they would launch their doomed attacks.

The ride was a long and lonely one.

And he could already feel his entire body aching.

It had been a long journey for him to get here—and only so that he might die in a land unknown, so many miles away from home.

He noted the slight uptake of pace among the troops; how their feet had grown quicker as bloodlust came to bear on their anticipation. They all wanted to be the first to cut open the skin of the enemy, to feel warm blood welling out of wounds.

But all they would really do—Rut was convinced—was *die*.

It was only as he watched the shadows peeling back before him—the gloom drawing back into itself—that he realised the single, solitary figure approaching them on the path ahead. He squinted as hard as he could.

Might this be another visit from the little girl?

Here to offer him a last nugget of wisdom, or advice?

Didn't she see that there was nothing to be done now . . . save for Rut's own assemblage of troops to retreat; and to be called cowards when they returned to Nor'tarth while all the others had been slain?

But it wasn't the little girl who appeared from out of the gloom. Not the little girl at all.

And Rut could hardly catch his breath to command his troops to hold their fire while he took in the sight; while he reasoned with himself who it *truly* was:

Hildie.

42

OUT OF DARKNESS, HEROES

HILDIE COULD FEEL the warm night air caressing her skin.

She breathed in the scent of the horses which began to encircle her, treating her like they might some mysterious rogue out in the wilderness who had the misfortune to cross paths with soldiers.

Her heart drummed lightly in her ears and she felt as if a creeping numbness was beginning to afflict her skin. She knew that her fire magic was tickling through her veins; and that, if she dared to allow it to take control of her, she could easily blow all these soldiers away—Rut among them.

If she truly wanted to escape from Shellacnass forever, this would be her perfect finale.

Let them write about that *in their history books!*

But she controlled herself.

She calmed her beating heart.

And the fire magic pumping through her.

Control was the important thing.

The only thing which separated her from the Creatures . . . or so said some mages.

Realising that the horsemen had now completely surrounded her, she decided that she needed to make her terms clear. That she needed to address them with the exact words and phrases which Inta had asked her to use.

So there would be no misunderstandings.

"The Horrox would like to announce a truce—an unconditional ceasefire."

Hildie eyed Rut, up high on his horse. His expression remained neutral. She knew that he had to play the leader here; that he no doubt had more to think about than merely the recovery of Hildie.

Over her shoulder, Hildie heard the sliding, teeth-grating sound of metal on metal as several troops drew their swords.

Were they planning to kill her now?

Was that the plan?

Had they weighed up all the factors and decided that Hildie was more of a threat than she was an asset?

Hildie held herself very still, aware that a single movement might set them off; might give them the wrong idea. But if they did believe that she would stand still while they executed her—while they did whatever it was they planned on doing—then they were gravely mistaken.

She shifted her gaze beyond the group who surrounded her and into the gloom which closed in on all sides. She knew the Horrox would be waiting for the soldiers.

That they would be prepared to strike them down.

This was going to be a massacre, and, despite the fact that Hildie wouldn't be the one wielding the killing force, she wouldn't feel any less responsible.

She could save the souls of all these men.

Feeling her voice harden in her throat, she turned to Rut and said, "Turn back! While you've still got time!"

Rut remained up on his horse, his thighs firmly grasping the flanks. He remained unmoving, almost as if he hadn't heard her command at all.

He *couldn't* make this about some sort of power game—as some sort of means to show that *he* was the one in charge . . . the one to make the decisions.

He surely knew what awaited these soldiers.

That the Horrox would *crush* them.

As Hildie stood between the horses, she felt Rut's gaze linger over her chest.

It took her a while before she realised that his eyes were fixed on the pendant which dangled down at her breast. At the Almber's Glass. That which Keeva had worn before.

Only then did Hildie realise how inappropriate it was of her to be wearing that which had belonged to Keeva; the body of whom had just that morning been deposited outside the town.

She waited for the reprimand.

Or, perhaps, the order for her immediate execution.

But it didn't come.

Several more moments of silence passed by, and Hildie felt the fire magic churn through her veins. She wanted to tell them whatever she could to make them understand—to make them understand that proceeding into the encampments would be nothing but suicide.

They *had* to turn back.

Rut clucked his tongue, urging his horse forward.

The troops followed his lead.

As Hildie stood there, in the middle of the plains, feeling as though she was thoroughly useless, she heard Rut utter, over his shoulder, "We'll see you back at the town—back at Nor'tarth."

While Hildie stood still, watching on as the mounted soldiers disappeared into the darkness, closing on the encampments, she wished that it might be true.

That they would come back alive.

Now the only question that remained was where *she* would go .

. .

43

RETURN

HILDIE HADN'T IMAGINED how it might be to return to Nor'tarth.

Perhaps she believed there would be a group of soldiers awaiting her, ready to lug her off to the gaols.

But, in reality, there was nobody standing guard.

From what she could tell, the entire garrison had been purged from the town; to go off and fight with the Horrox.

There must've been hundreds of them; hundreds who would never return home.

As Hildie trudged through the deserted cobblestone streets, she felt the flicker of torchlight warm her skin, and cause her fire magic to crackle about her veins. She knew that if she wished to quieten down her magic that she should leave the town behind and that she should go striding across the plains; in the moonlight.

To feel that chill in her blood once more.

Pinning her pride back down.

But, for some reason, she felt as if she should keep her magic operating at the very height of its power. That she couldn't afford to allow her defences to fall at this, the most fraught of times.

Because she could think of nowhere else to go, she plodded across the deserted town square and to Heffers Tavern, the lodgings where she had arrived with Rut on their first day in Nor'tarth.

It tickled her, as she crossed the threshold, to think that she had just as much money on her as the day she had arrived. She had nothing to exchange for so much as a bowl of broth; let alone for private quarters.

The front desk of the tavern, too, seemed somewhat solitary; now that it was devoid of Keeva ... of her *sister*.

Everything had happened so quickly, Hildie had learned so much about her father, that she still hadn't quite had time to process it all.

She wondered if she ever would completely.

The warmth from the tavern interior felt calming—*soothing*—against her skin, and she felt her heart giving percussive, squeezing beats as she stood in the main hall of the building; simply enjoying the sensation.

Perhaps she'd stood there for several hours—maybe it had been just a couple of minutes—when she heard a voice close by.

She turned her head to look. She saw, standing there, a grey-haired woman.

Several decades older than Hildie.

A *grandmother.*

Even before the woman said anything, Hildie knew who it was.

She knew that this was Keamard's wife.

Keeva's grandmother.

The woman had watery blue eyes. The bone structure of her face was fragile, and it seemed that her paper-white skin might bruise at the slightest of touches.

Hildie steeled herself, feeling that she was under just as much threat as if she had been waiting to face off with the most powerful of mages.

Before the woman got a chance to speak, Hildie managed to find the words.

"I'm sorry," she said. "I'm *so* sorry."

Strangely, almost out of nowhere, the woman gave her a gentle smile.

A smile *far* gentler than Hildie deserved.

The woman inclined her head slightly, in the direction of the staircase which led upward, apparently insinuating that Hildie was to follow.

And follow Hildie did.

44

THE ALMBER PROTECTORS

HILDIE FOLLOWED THE WOMAN—Keamard's widow —up the stairs of the tavern to a large room with oak panels. A single oil lamp sat on a table and illuminated the room. There were several well-padded armchairs and a pair of sofas which looked as though they'd been reclined upon by all and sundry.

The air in the room smelled dank and, when Hildie breathed in, she caught dust at the back of her throat. She held in her sneeze, though.

It seemed as though the fact that her mind remained fixed on the fate of Rut—and all those soldiers—prevented her from so much as breathing easily.

The woman sat down in one of the armchairs. She propped her elbow on the armrest and peered out through the window, down into the street below.

For the longest time, Hildie stayed on her feet, unsure about what she should do—what the *polite* thing would be to do.

Finally, she decided to perch on the edge of one of the sofas.

She stared at the elderly woman's face in profile, able to see certain similarities in her features; ones which Keeva had shared with her.

The finely poised nose.

The delicate jawline.

And the smooth angle of her neck running up the back of her head.

It felt almost as if Hildie had leaped forward in time, as if she had found herself facing off with Keeva many decades later.

As if she hadn't been slain by the Horrox.

When the woman finally did speak, Hildie found that she could hardly understand the words. She spoke at the level of a whisper and continued to peer out through the glass to the streets below. "I never did understand obsession—this monomaniacal desire to focus on just a single thing." Now she turned to look at Hildie; a slight smile sketched her lips. "There's so much beauty in this world for us to put on blinders; to refuse to see anything else."

Hildie's heart beat hard in her chest.

She felt the fire burning through her veins.

Tingling at her fingertips.

But now . . . now *wasn't* the time . . . she had made her choice, she had decided to return to Nor'tarth; to await her fate.

To see what the Mortals might do to her.

To see what her punishment might be.

"My husband," the woman continued, "he could never bring himself to leave this place—to go elsewhere." The smile grew larger and the creases became more engrained about the old woman's mouth and eyes. "I always wanted to see what Ilsnare might be like, what the *Crystal City* might hold in store." She shook her head. "But he was never the adventurous kind. The thought of visiting Almber's Bay—*his lifelong obsession*—never even crossed his mind. He knew that it was fraught with too much danger. What he was afraid of, I have no idea, because, as you saw well, he was never afraid of death. He was prepared to *die* for the Almber . . . and he did."

The woman's voice became almost too quiet to comprehend as she muttered the last words, and Hildie almost asked her to repeat herself.

But she had heard fine.

She had made out the words as clearly as she was able.

The woman drew in a profound breath, and then she sighed it back out again. She looked up at Hildie, that same smile lining her lips and yet with tears beginning to rise in her eyes.

More than anything, Hildie wished to get up from where she sat on the edge of the sofa; to go to the woman and wrap her arms about her. To tell her that everything would be okay.

But *how* would it be okay now that her husband and grand-daughter had been taken from her?

Quite simply, Hildie couldn't make those sorts of assurances.

They would've been a *lie*.

A single tear rolled down the woman's cheek, and she reached up—almost cursorily—and brushed it away with the back of her vein-stained hand.

The woman seemed to find some inner strength to continue.

"When I married my husband, my family left us this place"— she threw up her hands—"this *tavern*. You should have seen the look of joy in his eyes when he found out that he wouldn't need to soil his beautiful mind with something as rudimentary as *hard work*, that he could dedicate himself—*full-time*—to his passion; to the Almber." She gave a slight shake of her head. "He left me to administer the place, to balance the books, while he and my daughter—then our *granddaughter*—buried themselves in their research, and in their protection efforts."

Here Hildie could sense the woman getting into details that she would much rather not know. And yet, at the same time, she would scold herself later on for not having asked the question.

"Why did my father—Ma'reygar—slaughter the Almber?"

Again, a smile appeared on the woman's lips; the wrinkles becoming worn-in trenches. "Jealousy," she replied, a single-word answer apparently sufficing.

Hildie blinked several times, her heart quivering.

The woman shook her head. "No, your father, Ma'reygar, he couldn't cope with the fact that my daughter had another love; that she loved the *Almber* far more than she would ever love him . . . and so he decided to destroy them." She peered long and hard into Hildie's eyes. "Just as you yourself did."

Hildie wanted to protest, but the woman didn't pause, and her tone was insistent in a way which suggested that she wouldn't allow for interruption.

"But he should've known that there's no way of wiping out the Almber—not really." She dropped her tone and then added, "No matter how much some of us would like there to be."

Whatever the woman said, Hildie knew that things would be different this time; that whereas her father—such as had probably been his rage—might not have been thorough with carrying out his genocide; Hildie had incinerated the entire beach.

She had left nothing but Almber's Glass.

And a sole survivor.

With that thought on her mind, Hildie unconsciously reached for the necklace she wore, and which Keeva had worn; the pendant with the Almber's Glass.

She pulled it up over her head and offered it to the widow, but instead of reaching out to accept it, the widow simply shook her head.

"No," she said, her expression sober—*sincere.* "I have had enough, for me, as old as I might seem, this shall be a fresh start. A clean break."

As Hildie sat there, the Almber's Glass in her palm, she wondered at the weight of it; at how it felt as though it weighed a ton.

She wanted nothing other than to be as far away from the pendant as she could possibly manage. But she could hardly throw it away either.

Resigned to keeping it for the time being, Hildie tucked the pendant back inside the neck of her tunic and sank into the sofa; for the first time allowing the exhaustion to strike her.

For a long while, they sat in silence. When the woman finally raised her head, Hildie was certain that she was going to add some fresh titbit to the conversation; that she was going to leap in with some other nugget from the past which would further illuminate her father's true nature.

But, instead, she only said, "I can hear horses' hooves."

45

THE MONSTER WITHIN

R UT COULD FEEL the Horrox's dried blood all over his face.

Covering his armour.

Making it sticky.

It smelled thick and coppery—with a slight scent of rotten eggs clinging to it.

When he had chanced a look back over his troops, the ones who had followed him into the ambush, he had seen that they were all in a similar state. That their leather armour was coated in blood. That their *faces* were coated in blood.

Even as Rut felt the sure-footing of the cobblestones beneath his horse's hooves, he could still recall the feeling of arriving at the edge of the Horrox's encampments.

It had seemed wrong.

So wrong.

And yet he had given the silent gesture—the silent *order*—for his men to dismount and to take up their weapons. To approach the many darkened tarps and to *attack.*

Rut had been so convinced that it had been an attempt to trick them, to have them believe that they were asleep in their tents while—*secretly*—they watched on from the trees at a safe distance; ready to bring their magic to bear on the troops from Nor'tarth.

To bring their magic to bear on him.

But, no.

As Rut had thrust his sword downward, through the canvas of the tent, and into the form which lay curled up within, he had felt the hot blood come spurting out.

Covering him.

Almost like a comforting blanket against the chill of the night.

He had felt something shift inside him then.

Something which'd told him this was wrong.

That what he and his men were doing was just what the Horrox had done at Almber's Bay; how they had committed themselves to massacring that peaceable people.

And, what was more, Rut knew that he could never go back.

That he could never be who he had been before.

Innocence—if he had indeed still possessed it—deserted him now.

The previous battles he'd fought had all been for noble causes; for causes which were greater than himself. But this battle hadn't been a battle at all.

It was *unworthy* of being referred to in such terms.

It had been nothing short of a slaughter—a slaughter which had come into being following the bidding of Mortal powers.

After tonight, how could Mortals reasonably continue that old line about them being superior to Creatures? How could they go on denying the existence of magic throughout the kingdom when the evidence of it—when the *beauty* of it—was to be seen all around?

Rut had expected, as they had approached Nor'tarth from the plains—as they had returned from the Horrox encampments—that they would be greeted by the townspeople standing in their doorways; torches in their hands, smiles on their faces.

The long-hated enemy vanquished.

But, in reality, as Rut looked across the faces of the townspeople standing out on their doorsteps, he saw only a new sense of fear sketching their features.

They saw the blood.

The *black* blood.

And it covered their 'heroes'.

Rut led his troops on through the winding cobblestone streets, his horse seeming to know the way; or else his hands guided the reins without any intervention from his mind. His mind would remain—for days to come—back at the encampments; constantly sifting—and *resifting*—the memories of what he had witnessed.

He would never be able to blot all that blood from his brain.

Never be able to hide it from himself.

But, he supposed, neither *should* he.

Because that would be the true monster.

The monster within.

As Rut led the procession about the periphery of the town square, he turned his attention to the only prisoner they had taken. The only one of the Horrox who had shielded himself with his magic so that the Mortal swords—the Mortal arrows and bolts—would have no effect.

Why the others hadn't done the same escaped Rut.

The prisoner, as was the Mortal way, was held in his place with a frayed rope tied about his neck. He was guided along by a pair of soldiers on horseback, lightly padding along beside him.

They would make a spectacle of this now.

The townspeople would want to exact their revenge.

For all the terror that the Horrox had caused them; they would want to watch this Horrox put to death. They would want to watch him *suffer* for how he had made them feel.

As the soldiers kept the Horrox prisoner, Rut wondered why the Horrox didn't use his shapeshifting powers—or any of his *other* powers—to free himself from their Mortal hands.

But, then again, the Horrox had all allowed themselves to be killed in their beds.

And Rut couldn't help but believe that everything which had occurred here had been according to the Horrox's wishes.

On instinct, Rut turned his attention across the town square, and over to Heffers Tavern.

In one of the upper floors of the tavern, he saw a familiar face.

Hildie's face.

Peering out through the glass.

At least he had accomplished the quest Lou had assigned him.

At least he had done that much.

46

_____

A TOWN BREATHES EASY

HILDIE FELT HER HEART beating hard in her chest.

She felt the pendant with the Almber's Glass at the end of it rise and fall against her ribs.

She wished she had left it behind; back in her quarters.

In truth, she wanted to give it away; to never lay eyes on it again . . . and yet, inexplicably, until such a time occurred to her, she felt compared to wear it.

As she paced through the back lanes, she felt the sunrays warming her blood, making her feel stronger. More confident. That she had done the *right* thing.

What else *could* she have done?

If she had left the Horrox behind then the Horrox would've fought back.

They would've repelled the troops and then marched on Nor'-tarth, reducing the town to rubble with no mercy.

She had had no choice.

That much was obvious.

The whole town was deathly quiet at this time of the morning. The previous night, the mayor had declared today a day of rest; all the merchants could stay in bed. Craftsmen could down their tools.

And those who wished to do so could attend the execution.

The execution of Inta.

The only survivor of the slaughter of the Horrox the night before.

Hildie wondered if she would've gone to see him of her own volition. If she would've gone to see him before his execution, this morning. She wasn't certain either way. But the fact of the matter was that a manservant had come to her quarters at Heffers Tavern, passing on the message that Inta wished to see her.

She glanced to the doorway of the gaols, seeing the pair of soldiers standing there. One of them nodded her inside. Immediately, she was surrounded on all sides by cool stonework.

It wasn't too much of a challenge to find Inta. Soon after Hildie stepped into the gaols, a soldier arrived at her side, a kind of escort. He took it upon himself to—*silently*—guide her through the stone corridors, apparently in the direction of Inta's place of confinement.

Hildie found herself being hurried along, toward a single cell situated up several flights of winding stairs.

By the time she reached the top, she felt out of breath.

The soldier gave her a stern nod and he stood to attention over on the other side of the corridor, clearly not willing to allow Hildie and Inta to be alone.

Not that it mattered.

They didn't need to speak Mortal words with their tongues.

Not when they had their minds.

Hildie looked in through the bars of the gaol cell; a simple, stone arrangement with a tiny window which barely afforded a glimpse of the searing blue sky beyond.

Inta was sitting in the middle of the cell, his legs and arms crossed.

His head bowed.

If Hildie hadn't known so much about the Horrox—that they worshiped no gods—then she might've believed that Inta was praying for mercy. But, as became apparent when he tilted his head back to gaze at her, he had merely sunken into profound contemplation.

When he took her in, a faint smile lined his lips.

He spoke into her mind:

— *You're wearing the pendant. The pendant which belonged to your sister. The one which marks your father's great* destruction.

Hildie flinched and then tried to conceal her discomfort, looking away.

But she just managed to raise a measly reply within her own mind:

— *Yes. It's the burden I must bear.*

Feeling the soldier's intrusive gaze itch her skin, she decided that she needed to mask the true nature of their meeting with *some* Mortal words.

"How are you doing?" she said, and found herself wincing slightly at the question.

How did she *think* he was doing?

But, then again, what she said out loud really didn't have all that much importance.

She spoke to Inta within her mind.

— I'm so sorry. About what happened. About the way it happened. Horrifying.

Inta nodded to her in reply.

Then he answered her spoken words.

"I'm holding up fine," he replied, and then his smile widened. "This morning they were so kind as to serve me some gruel. When I pinched my nostrils it almost felt like I was chomping down porridge. Just like being home."

Hildie listened to the façade of conversation which Inta put up, and she couldn't help but notice the mournful tone to those final words: 'Just like being home'.

Then she turned her attention to the words which appeared directly in her mind.

The *real* words.

— You are not to blame. It had nothing to do with you. All it does is form another in the linked chain in the relations between Mortals and Creatures. It would only be 'horrifying' if nothing changes because of it. If my people; if I; die in vain.

Hildie felt a chill pass over the surface of her skin.

She thought back to their agreement.

That she would do the Horrox's bidding if only they would spare Nor'tarth.

And yet—*soon*—nobody except for herself and Inta would know of the promise ...

Apparently having read her thoughts, a fresh smile appeared on Inta's lizard-like mouth.

And he spoke into her mind again:

— Please, Hilda, your father might have been a great wizard but that doesn't mean that I haven't taken provisions to ensure that our

agreement *shall be properly put into place. That you shall uphold your end of the bargain.*

"What is my end of the bargain?" Hildie replied, speaking aloud without thinking, and right away flipping a glance off in the direction of the soldier standing nearby; afraid that he might've cottoned on to the true nature of the conversation.

But the soldier held tight to his spear, and kept his chin tilted up to the roof, apparently wishing to give the impression that his mind was someplace else.

That he had no interest in what Hildie and Inta spoke about.

All the same, she was certain he would relay every last detail to his superior once the meeting had reached its conclusion.

She had to take care.

Although it made her glad to think that this very day she and Rut would be leaving Nor'tarth behind, that they would be stepping onto Capital Road; headed for Ilsnare—the Crystal City— she also knew she would be treated with suspicion for the rest of her life.

And, perhaps, with good reason.

Finally, having allowed the dust to settle following her previous remark, Inta spoke into her mind once again:

—All we require of you is to serve our cause. We are shape shifters which is useful as far as it goes. But when it comes down to us wanting the equality we seek, we shall need more than simply Creatures by our sides. Having a mage of your power and influence to fight our cause could truly tip the scales. And, who's to say, you might not even need your magic; your influence with other persons of note could well prove enough to repay your debt to us.

To begin with, Hildie was so preoccupied with the concept that she was indebted to the Horrox—that she had *allowed herself* to become indebted to them—that she missed Inta's more subtle implication.

He knew about her history with Lou.

Knew her *feelings* for him.

The smile thickened on Inta's lips. She stared into those bottomless, black eyes.

Confirming her thought patterns, Inta gave her a nod.

She turned away from the bars. She glanced back at the soldier standing escort. Then she reached for the pendant hanging at her throat as if it might offer her some sort of divine protection.

As if she might be in need of some sort of divine protection.

"I'm ready to go now," she said, to the soldier.

The soldier straightened himself up then trod toward her, leading her on the way back down the corridor; away from where Inta was being held prisoner.

As she left Inta behind, she heard his voice one more time in her mind:

— *When the time is right; my people shall seek you out, Hildie, and you shall obey them. The fate of Nor'tarth depends on it. Do not be so foolish as to believe that there won't be many eyes in the darkness keeping track of your actions. This town shall breathe easily for the time being, but disaster; grave peril; shall never be far away. I can assure you of this. Let that pendant of yours provide you with a reminder of the* burden *you bear.*

47

LEAVING NOR'TARTH

HILDIE COULD FEEL the gentle, caressing breeze blowing across the plains which surrounded Nor'tarth. She felt the steady breathing of the horse beneath her; felt its steady, large movements between her thighs.

It was a long time since she had been on horseback, and—if there had been any other way—she wouldn't be so now.

But there had been no other practical measure.

No other way for them to reach Ilsnare by the fastest possible means.

Because, apparently, Hildie's presence in the Crystal City was a matter of urgency.

And the last thing she wanted to do was let down Louson Dorf —King of Shellacnass.

He might have her executed . . . just as the townspeople of Nor'tarth had decided to have Inta executed.

She was glad to have left the town behind without having to

witness the execution; that would've been too grim. She had seen enough horror in the past few days to last her through the foreseeable future. Why was it that she had spent such a peaceful, uneventful decade out in the wilderness—far away from her past—and only now, when she had allowed her past back in, the horror had begun again?

And that same horror trapped her now.

Because, if she didn't play her role—if she didn't do as she was instructed; by the condemned Inta, and by Louson Dorf, King of Shellacnass; she would be simply brushed aside by fate; her life crushed like an insignificant ant beneath a boot heel.

When Hildie had declared to Rut that she didn't wish to stay around the town to witness the execution, she had sensed the relief pour out of him.

That he was glad not to witness the execution.

From the sound of things, there was enough terror awaiting them in the near future that they should make an effort to ward it away in the immediate present.

The two of them cut solitary figures; both on horseback, both of them trotting along the dirt track in silence. Both of them lost within their own thoughts.

As Hildie followed Rut's lead, she was aware of the sudden shouts which reverberated in their wake; surely the townspeople celebrating the murder of Inta, and, more to the point, the vanquishing of the threat which'd loomed large over the town for the past few weeks.

Now Mortals could go back to believing that they were the dominant force throughout Shellacnass; and that they were the only ones worthy of governing the land.

If only they knew the truth.

If only they thought to look just a little beyond the tips of their own noses.

Then they might see.

The cries died down behind them, and Hildie turned herself around in her saddle to face the dirt track ahead. To look into her future.

Thinking about it now, she realised that the promise she had made with Inta, the one which had seen Nor'tarth spared, meant that it would be her job to make Mortals see.

To make them realise that equality, that the freedom to be seen all about the kingdom, was something which should be made a basic right for all Magical beings.

Perhaps then Hildie's magical powers might be celebrated, rather than called upon by sordid, underhanded means; as if to invoke her abilities was nothing more than a glorified failure. Hadn't Louson once proven that he was the most powerful mage in the land?

Why should he need *Hildie's* aid?

Why should he need *anybody's* aid?

As Hildie thought more and more on the situation she found herself in, she could hardly believe that only weeks before she had been living a tranquil life with the Almber; unaware of her own past connections to them, those most unfortunate connections which her father had forged for her. Even now, when she thought on the Almber, she knew she would find nothing of the peace she had had.

How could she think of peace when she knew how it had ended?

When she knew what she had done?

Hilda, daughter of Ma'reygar, the *Perennial* Destroyer; that, surely, would be her epitaph.

Hildie felt her horse stirring uneasily beneath her, and she turned her mind to other matters. She realised that she must've been tensing her muscles, unconsciously tightening her hold on the reins; sinking the bit deeper into the corners of the horse's soft mouth.

She never wanted to harm any living creature.

She had been an innocent girl once, too.

But she never would be again.

Hildie stared at the dirt path up ahead, as if weaved its way through the long grasses of the plains. She watched how the path lifted up over the hillside. Soon she and Rut would be climbing that slope. The two of them. A most unlikely pair of travelling companions.

But needs must.

It was strange to think, after everything the two of them had gone through these past few days, that Hildie still hadn't much caught up with Rut's life. That she didn't know anything of his life.

While they'd never been close, she would certainly have had the nerve to call him 'friend' in the past.

And although he wasn't *that* right at the moment, she was determined to change it.

From the looks of things, she would need all the friends she could get when she arrived to Ilsnare.

Several days—if not *weeks*—of travel lay ahead of them.

Time enough to learn about one another.

Time enough to grow comfortable.

Time enough to *trust*?

Hildie glanced to Rut, took in his doughy face, and the blond hair which hung down in unkempt corkscrew curls. He looked weary; the dark circles beneath his eyes gave him away. He looked a man who had the world weighing down his shoulders.

It was almost as if he sensed her, as if he experienced that same tingle across the surface of the skin which Hildie had when she realised someone was watching her.

He turned his head. His eyes skimmed over hers.

Light blue.

Seemingly free of cares.

So different from the pit-black eyes of the Horrox.

And Hildie's own sea-green set.

He held her gaze for several moments, and then, his focus slipped downward; to her throat. To where the pendant hung at the end of its golden chain.

For the longest time, he continued to stare, as if he had become bewitched by the item.

Hildie wondered at the effect for several moments. Then, without warning—as unexpected as anything else in the late-morning light—with the sounds of the crowds baying for blood having grown silent on their heels, Rut raised his attention back to her face.

And flashed her a smile.

For that moment, Hildie saw the happy-go-lucky Rut she had always known.

Who she was determined to know again.

She returned his smile.

And felt the warmth rise up to her heart.

Perhaps there *was* still time for her.

Time for her to find her place in the world.

48

ALMBER'S BAY

THE SEA SWEPT into the beach of Almber's Bay, bringing with it a multitude of pebbles and countless grains of sand. The sun beamed down onto the tropical shallows, bringing out a brilliant-blue glow from the crystal-clear water. The air smelled of bananas, and of pineapples, of all the nearby tropical fruits; ripe for picking and yet untended-to ever since the Almber had gone . . . ever since the Almber had been wiped out.

A little girl appeared on the shore—seemingly out of the thick, humid air itself.

Her long walnut-coloured hair and coffee-coloured skin made her stand out against the fine, blond sands. And yet she didn't seem to be out of place . . . to be a stranger in a strange land.

No, she belonged here.

That much was obvious.

The wind caught her long hair and it tussled over her face. She had to claw it free from her eyes; tuck it back behind her ears. A smile lined her pert lips and a sparkle shimmered off the surface of her eyes.

She took a single step and years seemed to pass by.

Not so much the beating of a pendulum—*back and forth; back and forth*—more like the constant spinning of a clock's hands about the face.

Clouds bundled up overhead. Storms blew themselves in.

And blew themselves out.

As the girl continued to stride forward, making for the shoreline, her limbs grew longer.

Her hair reached her waist.

And her face lost its softness and her jaw took on severe, feminine, handsome lines.

She became a woman.

When the sea first caressed the tips of her toes, her stomach began to swell.

Her entire body seemed to swell.

Because she was carrying a civilisation.

One which—*one day*—would rise and occupy Almber's Bay.

Just as it had done for all the aeons.

All over again.

When the woman turned away from the sea, when she left its shallows behind, her mind already fixated on building shelter, she rested her hand on the crest of her belly and, although it was almost imperceptible, she felt a kick . . . the first sign of life of a new civilisation.

Growing within her.

Ready to be born.

Ready for the world.

All the sadness, all the tragedy . . . but this time—*this time*—it might be different.

And, whatever happened, it would be beautiful.

There was no doubt about it.

For however long it lasted.

AUTHOR'S NOTE

Thank you for taking the time to read one of my books. If you would like to hear about my latest releases you can sign up for my newsletter here: www.raymondsflex.com

Thanks for reading!

Raymond S Flex

Heart Of Flame
The Fifth Crystal Kingdom Novel

Copyright © Raymond S Flex, 2015.
Published by DIB Books
All rights reserved.

Cover design and layout copyright © DIB Books, 2015.
Cover art copyright © Andriy Zholudyev & Mopic / Shutterstock, 2015.

This work is fictional. None of the characters or events depicted in this book are based on real life and any resemblance to real events or persons is purely coincidental.
Neither this book, nor any part of it, may be reproduced without express permission from the publisher.

All rights reserved.

www.ingramcontent.com/pod-product-compliance
Lightning Source LLC
Chambersburg PA
CBHW031219260626
47169CB00007B/2110